Karen Testa was born in Ohio, USA and grew up in Richmond, Virginia. Currently she works in England and lives in Hampstead where she and her husband share their flat with one aloof house cat.

Happy Like
BARNACLES
KAREN TESTA

A Touchstone Book
Published by Simon & Schuster
New York   London
Toronto   Sydney
Tokyo   Singapore

First published in Great Britain by Touchstone Books, 1994
An imprint of Simon & Schuster Ltd
A Paramount Communications Company

Simon & Schuster Ltd
West Garden Place
Kendal Street
London W2 2AQ

Simon & Schuster of Australia Pty Ltd
Sydney

A CIP catalogue record for this book is
available from the British Library

ISBN 0-671-71844-4

Typeset in Sabon by
Hewer Text Composition Services, Edinburgh
Printed and bound in Great Britain by
Harper*Collins* Manufacturing, Glasgow

Acknowledgements

My thanks and gratitude to the following people: Sloan Alday, Jim Dillon, Alex Gourlay, Hugh Hamilton-Meikle, and Lia Jeans — for patience and literary insights above and beyond the call of common friendship. And to my family for constant encouragement — Susan Dailey, Everett Kilmer, David Testa, and the two Adenas!

For Peter, and for Mom and Dad,
because all of you said that I could.

M orton Penmen Maverin IV hailed from a long and pompous line of hearty Southern males who passed down their name as an heirloom more coveted than great-granddaddy's julep cups. After all, the name was durable, and drinking vessels were not. During America's War Between the States, the Maverins had sorrowfully, but with a delicious feeling of self-sacrifice, melted down their julep cups to make bullets. Or so Morton Penmen Maverin IV told the tale. He did not have to tell us, his listeners, that the resultant bullets were purest silver, because great-granddaddy's julep cups undoubtedly would have been silver — heavy, hand-molded sterling. The kind of silver which, despite its thickness, would quickly transfer the chill of shaved ice and bourbon to the smooth Southern palm of a gentleman drinker.

The ancestors of Morton Penmen Maverin IV had considered julep cups a small sacrifice for the Rebel cause. In modern times, similar manly martyrdoms might be asked in preservation of the family name. Our friend, the fourth Morton, lived under a polite paternal warning that he would be castrated before he could participate in the creation of a male child christened anything other than Morton Penmen Maverin V. Our Penmen shivered often and dreamed of children named Edward.

We around the fire called him Penman, partially for the pleasure of knowing him and loving him enough to name him ourselves, and partly because of his artistic bent. Maybe names really do aid in molding our personalities. Sometimes I saw Penman in my head as The Pen Man, with a flowing quill and a head which erupted hourly with story ideas. Penman could write; dismal things, sometimes, which reflected his diet of morbid movies. His best writing, however, surfaced in essays which happened when he isolated something around him and just stared at it.

One day early in our time together, Penman peered at our house cat, holding her eye contact until she, annoyed at an invincible opponent, went to her litter box and vented her frustration in a vehement spray of chlorophyll bits. The essay Penman wrote on kitty served as the beginning of his profitable connection with a major magazine. Penman's parents displayed amazement at his writing talents; they never expected him to be useful. To his dismay, Penman's relatives value the family name even more highly now that it appears frequently on the thick white pages of a national magazine.

While other people *talk*, Penman *pontificates*. When the rest of our race *fibs*, Penman *prevaricates*. I am convinced that at some point in his earlier existence, Penman ate an entire *Oxford English Dictionary*, unabridged, and has yet to recover. Like the fashionable dresser who wears all his finery at one time, Penman is a word dandy.

Oddly enough, it was Penman's vocabulary which brought the six of us together back when we were freshmen at a tiny university in North Carolina. On the first day of term each of us had been drawn, one by one, to a table in the dining hall where Penman held court. He was calling for a languid mutiny.

'Excrement . . . I wasn't raised to ingest excrement, and unless you were bred in a family of exotic dung beetles, you really must join me in refusing to eat excrement. Assuredly I don't expect *salmon en croute* or tender chateaubriand, but, please.' At this juncture Penman stood and held out his hands in a gesture both elegant and beseeching. 'Let us admit that this is harvest of the septic tank and not *boeuf bourgignon*. My fellow collegians, perhaps we should unite. We have nothing to lose but our rather insignificant little lives.'

After those words we all sat down at Penman's table: Marjorie, Nathan, Katherine, Miles and I. Marjorie sat because she and Penman had been friends for years; she had not followed him to the same university merely to desert Penman at the first instance of his making an ass of himself. Nathan settled with Penman because he relished revolution. Katherine arose from the table at which she had been sitting because no one there shared her outrage at finding a human hair entwined in the tines of her fork; she wished to couple her indignation with Penman's indigestion. Miles approached the group because he enjoyed complaining. And I followed, though I will never know why. It has long been my role to watch and listen. Penman calls me an energy voyeur.

Throughout our four years at university the six of us remained cronies, an unusual thing even on our intimate campus. As much as people can belong to each other, I would say we do. We have shared everything from textbooks to horribly scabby cases of adult chicken pox in our senior year. It was while Nathan, Miles, and I scratched at our sores and Katherine shrieked at us to stop, that Penman suggested we all live together for one year after university. Because our companionship formed the habit of our days it did not occur to any of the six of us to dissent. And real life offered nothing so pressing that we could not sidestep it for 365 days.

Lack of dissent formed the beginning of a trail which ended right here, with Penman, Marjorie, Katherine, Nathan, Miles, and me settled around a tiny driftwood fire in the den of our beach house. Weighty and humid, the atmosphere of a coastal Virginia twilight settled over us like meringue. Even our tiny fire added heat, very unwelcome heat. But the infant August night would be oppressive with or without the coloured flames, and we enjoyed the thought of gathering around a hearth.

Because all six of us lounged around the fire, no one noticed my silence. Six is a good number for a group; with six, someone always feels chatty and someone else mellow. I suppose seven, though, would be the perfect number for a discussion. Then everyone could range up and down the talkative gradient like the acid half of a Ph scale. Tonight, with our imperfect Ph, I was a seven for neutral silence and Penman was a one for loud and obnoxious. Penman had begun talking whilst leaning on the back of a sofa, but at some point he had oozed over it, and come to rest in a sort of personal puddle next to Marjorie. She regarded him with distaste. On Marjorie distaste manifests itself with an infinitesimal lift of one eyebrow. The lift of her eyebrow causes one eye to open slightly more than the other, and the perfect symmetry of her face is diminished.

'Penman,' she said, adding a small lip quiver to the movement of her eyebrow. 'It's very well to play the bohemian aesthete, but when are you going to bathe again? You smell of decay.'

Ignoring her, Penman drank from Marjorie's beer. We all watched as the liquid in the barrelish green bottle drained away, then Marjorie spoke serenely. 'Penman, you perpetual piece of hell, go and get me another.'

Penman headed off for the refrigerator and left us, five around the fire. By nearly imperceptible degrees, Marjorie's face reverted to its standard lack of expression. She looked at each one of us in turn before saying, thoughtfully, 'Penman is an ass.'

Marjorie's words possess a force of authority that comes from the quiet certitude with which she offers them. She is a philosopher, both by nature and study, and we respect her for knowing the ideas of men whose names we massacre in pronouncing. From sources as diverse as Anselm to greeting cards she collects the ideas she finds useful and allows the rest to percolate through her peaceful head and out of her thoughts forever. Marjorie lives her life in a seldom-ruffled calm impervious to mental whitecaps.

To the delight of her society family, Marjorie appears oddly beautiful, with eyes that affirm the calm of her thoughts and skin to rival the smoothness of a professionally concocted *beurre blanc*. By design, actresses and models seldom smile or frown, thereby seeking to avert the lines which ordinary facial expressions erode in skin. Marjorie's lack of expression is unaffected. I have never heard her raise her voice. Though she knows us all intimately, she and Penman are symbiotic. Their relationship defies any conventional description, so perhaps it won't seem inappropriate to describe their friendship in a culinary metaphor: Penman is the yeast and Marjorie the flour in a mixture which makes bread without heat. No heat because neither one sees the other romantically. The notion of a kiss would be more uncomfortable than an enema.

On an earlier warm evening in August, when we had been similarly and inappropriately settled around a tiny fire to enjoy the driftwood flames, Marjorie told us of the history she shared with Penman.

'Since we were six, we've lived only five doors apart.' That was misleading considering that in the aristocratic outskirts of Richmond, Virginia, the big old houses have 100 acre estates which flounce out from the main structures like full skirts. Marjorie's family considered Penman's family neighbours even though they lived two miles apart. We were not impressed.

'We were in the same kindergarten class at Grace and Holy Trinity Church. I liked Penman because he didn't like orange. On the second day of school we made a pact to chew up our orange crayons, and, having chewed up our own, we went on to rid the whole class of orange crayons. Right around Halloween, the other kids got out their stubby black crayons and went searching for their orange ones. It was a triumphant moment. Do you remember?'

Penman only looked at her vaguely and remarked that the crayon companies had quite a little marketing strategy going on. Since individual colours aren't sold separately, people have to buy whole new sets in order to replace a single lost colour. Having delivered himself of his corporate commentary, Penman stretched and offered that orange crayons and carrots rated equally badly in his world view. Penman is the only adult I have ever met who absolutely refuses to eat vegetables, and who rounds out that fourth food group with large quantities of home-made guacamole dip.

'Marjorie,' said Penman, 'I remember little about that year beyond our decision that we were both aliens with long curly antennae which were easily bent. Ducking through all those door frames cramped my back terribly.'

'Did you know that you were a bit odd for your age?' Typically, it was Katherine who asked that. Her practical nature spends much time figuring out what's weird and what's normal and whether or not any of us suit her definitions. Katherine deferred medical school for a year so that she could come and live with us while we deferred business and law school and other graduate degrees. Some of our parents wondered if we were actually deferring on life. Some others thought it was wise of us to live *life* before we disappeared into the relatively sequestered worlds of our chosen professions. My father, who engineered his own rise in the banking world, told us all bluntly: 'learn to wait on other people. When it comes your turn to be waited upon, as it will after these hellatious pricey educations, you will know how to treat those who serve you.' So we were cocktail waitresses and bar backs, pizza makers and receptionists not just because the tips accrued quickly, but because someday we'd appreciate being served, because we had once been the servers.

For this year of grace, Katherine's job involves bringing drinks to people at a raucous bar. A typical doctor's daughter, Katherine began her cocktail career by delivering health warnings with every drink. Her lack of tips became noteworthy. After considerable soul-searching, she reluctantly allowed economics to curb her ethics. The experience has turned into a life lesson for Katherine; she has very nearly learned the incalculably valuable skill of clamping her jaw shut and smiling silently. Undoubtedly, such reticence pains her horribly. We all live our lives according to creed, whether or not we've bothered to translate our personal creeds into words. In my imagination Katherine's life motto hangs around her throat, like the chains which circle the necks of decanters to identify each bottle as 'gin', 'brandy' or 'cognac'. Katherine's neck tag says 'I nag, therefore I am'.

Her unsuspecting customers never know that their tipping habits and idle tête-à-têtes are being dissected constantly by her analytical brain. Katherine has to think all the time or her brain gets tired. My sister, a marine zoologist, says that sharks have to swim all the time to avoid exhaustion. What might otherwise be a titbit of bio-chemical trivia becomes the basis for an extended metaphor when I consider Katherine's appearance. Tall and lean, with a minimum mainte- nance hairstyle and an intense expression, strangers find Katherine daunting.

Katherine's doing some research into her current mental fixation – sexual psychology – and many of her theories get tried out on us. Penman and Marjorie present a fascinating study for Katherine, and they kindly stage shows for her amusement. The most recent theory showcases platonic male/ female relationships. Katherine is absolutely certain that homosexual leanings develop from the kind of compatibility Penman and Marjorie enjoy. Once I sat down to listen to her explain it. Unfortunately, I was simultaneously involved in doing the household accounts and shovelling in an odious package of banana yoghurt that was due to expire the next morning, so I don't remember much of Katherine's theory. It has something to do with taking on male or female qualities to identify more closely with your friend of a different sex. So in this case, Penman takes on feminine qualities to identify with Marjorie, and Marjorie takes on masculine qualities to identify with Penman. The only fault I see in all this is that while Marjorie takes on a masculine role, Penman busies himself taking on a feminine role, so the two never really get a chance to identify with each other because one is always masculine and the other feminine. Does this make sense? Perhaps there is more to Katherine's theory than I gather.

Anyway, Marjorie has been putting her underwear in Penman's laundry, and Penman puts his Y-fronts in Marjorie's dirty clothes basket. Katherine always does the laundry for everyone because no one else separates the lights and darks correctly, and she can't stand seeing us all in grey apparel that began life as white. Emerging from the laundry room, Katherine looks smug and vindicated. Marjorie and Penman look at each other and smile.

While Marjorie and Penman ought to view each other romantically and don't, Katherine and her boyfriend Nathan do but should not. Shortly after meeting in freshman year, Katherine and Nathan began to date each other exclusively. No one knows why. Possessing enough hair so that people who see him for the first time in the winter months wonder if he has emerged early from some cave, Nathan resembles a kindly Kodiak bear. He likes his clothes grey and everything else black and white. Principally, Nathan is a statesman, the Ghandi type who will lead populist masses into nirvanas where animals are mercifully killed for food purposes only and no one ever goes hungry or spiritually unsatisfied. On a night when all of us have gotten good tips and humanity seems wonderful, Nathan can shape a wave with words that we all want to ride. He has spurred us to write letters for Cambodian prisoners of conscience and to demonstrate publicly for continued aid to Ethiopia. His optimism that the rational intelligence of mankind will pervade in all social and economic issues is more infectious than herpes. It doesn't hurt that he debated on a national level and has a quiet blunt speaking style which stops potential dissent more effectively than a mouth full of bean sprouts.

Since early childhood, Nathan has had diabetes. Everyone he knows worries about him far more than he does. Though he just about manages to take his insulin shots regularly, Nathan's exercise, sleeping habits, and diet are nothing if not spastic. His job for our year at the beach involves every possible duty at a nearby Pizza Hut. When he's not working, Nathan either helps out at a soup kitchen in neighbouring Hampton, or waxes his surfboard, in preparation for learning how to use it.

Katherine and Nathan seldom meet except on late, late evenings when they have both finished work and they sit triple layer on an old chair in our den. In other words, Katherine perches on Nathan's lap and on Katherine's lap perches a 'mistake' pizza that Nathan brings home. The three of them commune until the wee hours. Early in the morning, one of us usually comes downstairs to find the tri-level tower collapsed into Nathan and Katherine curled on the couch with a dead pizza box. Penman once regarded the two long bodies tangled on the couch and mused on the odds on Katherine being strangled by Nathan's hair.

After five years together, however, the likelihood of Nathan snuffing out the essential elements of Katherine, or vice versa, seems remote. Just as the flight of a bumblebee is impossible — according to the laws of physics — but ultimately successful, so are Nathan and Katherine. I won't venture to comment on their biomechanics, but psychologically, they form a strange but sure pair. A pair unique in that neither of them has succeeded in changing the other in any way at all.

Only once has Nathan ever spoken to me about his relationship with Katherine. At the time we were out jogging, because my ice-cream thighs perturbed me and his looming beer belly worried him. Independently, Nathan and I had made our resolutions to exercise. But as we ran at night, along rural roads, it made sense to run together. I remember his words perfectly, punctuated as they were by puffs of curried breath; that was the year when Nathan discovered lentils with fiery Indian seasonings.

'Do I love Katherine? – huff – what a question.'

'Are you going to answer me?' I asked him. 'Or will I have nothing from you but your pungent exhale?'

'Do you realize that love is but a quantitative term so that other people can – huff – measure the depth of my feelings – huff huff. If you realize that, then you'll understand when I say that I love Katherine – huff – because she doesn't expect me to have time for her. And Katherine loves me because – huff – I don't expect her to have time for me. We value ourselves highly. By conventional definitions, that's not love.'

That was the day I learned that Nathan, too, wore the badge of his life creed around his neck, and the badge said 'Let me be'.

Though Katherine and Nathan have very little of harmony in their life together, they don't seem to care. Katherine nags, and Nathan baits her. Upon entering a restaurant, Katherine sniffs for disinfectant. Nathan, meanwhile, shakes out his tresses and comments absently on the possibility that Third World countries could use the hair on their collective heads to cultivate a new breed of edible lice. I imagine Katherine and Nathan as two magnets of equal strength; joined together properly, the attraction is fierce. Wrong way around, however, the opposition of the two magnets gives each exceptional vivacity.

If love were rational and like sought like, Katherine would join not with Nathan, but Miles. Which would leave me by myself. Though Nathan and I are very close, we are not physically suited to each other. Back in freshman year, the six of us attempted various romantic relationships before settling into a pattern. Miles, the most practical and mathematical among us, figured out that 720 permutations and combinations loomed as possibilities between the six of us. I watched and saw that Miles' comment interested Katherine and made Marjorie ascend an eyebrow. Penman snorted, while Nathan suggested that if we were going to attempt a *ménage à* sextuplets, he did not wish to be the one on the bottom. Abandoning his arithmetic, Miles agreed with Nathan.

For four years I have spent a sizeable chunk of each day with Miles. Trying to be objective about him is like trying to be objective about a puppy – with floppy ears, big paws and bright eyes – which steadfastly refuses to become house-trained. I can describe better how Miles relates to all of us than how he relates to me. If the six of us were a salad bar, Miles would be the beets, and, like beets, you either love him or hate him. Marjorie says Miles is charmingly irascible. Nathan says he is a tightwad. Penman says Miles is both the subtly spiced lobster thermidor dinner and the unpleasant acid belch which follows it. Katherine thinks Miles is a Yankee neurosis. At any rate, he is better characterized by himself than by anything we can say about him.

Something sizzled in the fireplace and we peered at the glowing lumps with interest. Marjorie, as chief collector of driftwood for the fire, had the most authority to speak on the subject of what sizzled in the flames.

'Live barnacles,' said Marjorie.

'And how does one separate the quick from the dead in the world of the barnacle?' Miles asked.

'It's not easy.' Marjorie sipped from her fresh beer and looked thoughtful – a matter of lowering her eyelids to half mast. 'I'm not exactly sure what life means to a barnacle, or an earthworm, or a slug.'

Katherine cringed at the mention of slugs. Sea air makes our house a damp one, and trails of silvery slime lace both the old wooden boards and our very 1970s orange shag carpets. Nathan and Miles handle the slug disposal. While Nathan prefers to salt them, Miles sets out bowls of beer to entice the little blobs into drowning. Neither solution has affected the slugs' numbers in the slightest, and both solutions bring Katherine to a frenzy. Salt makes of slugs slippery mounds on the floor, and bowls of beer create containers of a stew that Katherine can't bear to empty. As a last resort we've scattered slug pellets everywhere, only to find that we possess a sturdy breed which views slug pellets as rest stops.

'Given my skeletal knowledge of biological anatomy,' Marjorie interrupted herself to smile minimally at Katherine, 'I know that the barnacle has a very limited nervous system. And I doubt whether its limited nervous system allows for instinct. But I think long ago a gift was made to small stupid things. The gift is specific instructions, a knowing what to do. Every simple species received that gift and the few skills needed to implement such a gift. Small stupid things wish only to follow their instructions. If happiness does indeed occur to a barnacle, it occurs when it has fastened itself to something. Barnacles are sad only when free.'

'Marjorie, you must allow me to issue you with abundant congratulations. You have solved all the barnacle's dilemmas by incinerating it.' Penman continued looking at the fire while he edged closer. He admires all the tiny licking colours in a driftwood blaze, and sits so close that he worries Katherine. At my parents' home I have a huge black dog called Marvel, who places her front paws near the grate and leans in toward the flames regardless of the heat. Pyro puppy. Pyro Penman.

'Hey,' said Nathan from above the backgammon board over which he and Miles hunched. 'Did anyone have to ask specially to get tonight off, or is this simply a coincidence?'

We were all just lucky. It's most likely that only two or three of us will be home together on any given night. Very seldom do four of us have the evening off, and this evening, with all six of us home, was a first. Katherine had been due to work tonight, but early in the afternoon she received a call from her manager, who said that one of the grills in the kitchen had caught fire and gutted 'the goddamn place'.

'So,' Katherine told us, triumphantly, 'no Kudzu

Cafe for the rest of the week. Though I can't have any compensation for lost tips, I made sure that I'll still receive my hourly wage. After all, it's not *my* fault that some fool never cleaned the filters in those grill exhausts. The oily build-up there has been a fire hazard for years. Twice last week I made warning comments to the cook.'

I caught Marjorie's eye and saw with amusement that it had rolled up toward the ceiling. Back in position, the eye gazed blandly while Katherine continued speaking. 'Perhaps I'll have time to outgrow my lycra uniform.' Penman snorted and told her that one never outgrew lycra, one just bulged in other than the usual places.

'I have never in my life bulged,' said Katherine, craning her neck until the sinew showed. 'The only things sticking out of my uniform are my hip bones. And my panty lines, apparently. Do you know, the manager told me to stop wearing underwear because the lines showed?' Ever since Katherine began her job at the Kudzu Cafe, we have heard about the lycra bicycling shorts which comprise the lower half of her uniform. She says that tight shorts engender infection and can cause sterility in males. I decided to intervene before Katherine began a verbal treatise on crotch rot.

'What are we having for dinner? I'm feeling feisty for food, and we may as well dine *en masse* since we're all here. Who feels like crab?' I asked only to get the discussion going. Trying to reach a decision about what to eat is difficult even for two people. The difficulty increases by exponents according to how many people are present. Thus we were at two to the fourth power difficulty and it was already seven p.m. I wanted a decision by eight-thirty when the seafood store closed. Given the usual course of events, we would be just in time.

'No live crabs,' said Miles. He meant what he said. Last week he went by himself to pick up his first bushel of crabs. Normally, Nathan or I go down to the docks and pick up a bushel of steamed crabs — definitely, deliciously, dead. After Miles' inaugural visit to the docks, however, he returned flushed and worried with a huge dripping box full of snapping, bubbling, hissing, hard shells. Miles' crabs were alive, formidably so. We had no idea what to do. I went out to the porch with them, and, from a safe distance, watered the creatures down with a hose while Miles frantically consulted a cookery book. After three hours of continuous cursing we had succeeded in steaming a total of seven dozen crustaceans. Marjorie came home midway through the whole ordeal and took silent stock of our expletives, our steam burns, and claw marks. She hauled the rest of the crabs back to the ocean; they would have died slowly while waiting their spot in the pot.

Two days later we were still eating crab. Penman smothered the leftover crabs in a homemade hot pepper crab boil which made sweat pop out of my forehead. The recipe, he said, came from his mother, a no-nonsense New Orleans Belle who grew up on crayfish boiled in the stuff. Miles tasted the mixture and said that the Southerners stole it from the Yankees to use as gunpowder in the Civil War.

Tonight, perhaps for the best, no one felt like crabs. In the way of seasonal feasts, we had gorged too often, and crabs had lost their initial appeal. Penman announced that picking crustaceans was too much effort for too little sustenance.

'Not just that,' said Katherine, 'but have you considered the amount of toxins that crabs absorb by crawling along in sea sludge.' No, we hadn't.

Shrimp was the next suggestion. Nathan objected politely.

'Ever since we started the shrimp and tuna pizza at work, I get these furry pimples on my lips whenever I eat shellfish.' Imagining furry lips, we fell silent for a moment.

'I'd like to see that sometime,' said Marjorie, finally. Nathan bared his teeth at her as the search for a mutually suitable food continued.

Katherine won't eat beef.

Nathan hates fish.

Penman likes lobster.

Miles just wants lots, cheaply.

Marjorie was in an herbal tea mood.

The interesting thing was that if it were necessary, all of us could sit down to any fixed menu and eat respectable portions of each course. We are all adult enough when we have no choice. The problem was that tonight we had a choice, and we work very hard for our money. Therefore, we were all determined to eat very well of whatever we liked. Katherine as usual dealt with the complex issue most efficiently. She wedged the six of us into her car and took us to the Grey Gull where we ordered take-out.

After we ordered we sat at the bar and had margaritas while waiting for the kitchen to produce our dinners. Penman went to a fish tank to eye the lobsters judiciously. Marjorie soon joined him, and I heard him demand that she tell him what makes lobsters happy. Marjorie smiled at him serenely. 'Eating barnacles. Time for another margarita, Penman. These margaritas are an excellent source of enlightenment.'

Marjorie sees things whenever her intake of alcohol rises over a teaspoon. We can always tell when the pink pachyderms have come out to play because she stays quieter, even, than usual, and her eyes move to follow imaginary objects. Most of the time the real and the drink-induced remain clearly defined. The only time she has ever been unsure was when she was sixteen and she had her first glass of champagne at a dinner to celebrate her brother's impending nuptials. She says her elderly Uncle Richard, with his short puff of white hair atop a thin tubular head, turned into an electric blender right before her eyes. She justified Uncle Richard's transformation by saying that his hair resembled the foam on a vanilla milkshake, and his head and neck shared the shape of Warings' best blender.

Marjorie has seen things at all our festive occasions. The Gnomemobile discharged guests at her twenty-first birthday fête. After a cup of eggnog two years ago, her Christmas tree sprouted Japanese lanterns. Kafka came to our party of New Year 1990. Tonight she saw . . . 'Girl Scouts'. Marjorie nearly fell off her bar stool as she peered intently into the main dining room. 'Girl Scouts are serving dinner in there. I don't need another margarita.'

Our seafood was ready halfway through Miles' second bowl of the complimentary salt and vinegar potato chips on the bar. Taking our bags, we prepared to troop out onto the beach.

'Has everyone washed their hands?' wondered Katherine.

'You're not my mother, damnit,' said Miles. 'When you say stuff like that I feel like sticking my hands in the cat's litter box then kneading you some bread.'

'*Sans* an interlude of hand washing, I presume.' Penman added obligingly.

Bickering, Miles and Katherine fell to the rear as we headed out to Chicks Cove beach. Eating on the ocean shore is the best alternative I know to using napkins. After making messes we just dive into the water and wash juices, spices, and lemon butter away from wherever they have dripped. Katherine won't allow us to use paper napkins because she says they are a poor use of wood pulp. Early in our sojourn together at the beach, Nathan suggested that we each get a big dog to lick our fingers at mealtimes, thereby re-creating medieval habit and hygiene for our own table. Katherine ignored him and bought cloth napkins. Penman approved. He thought paper napkins were vulgar.

I did not feel twenty-three years old. Looking around at all of us, eating and chortling and chatting, I wondered whether we looked like adults to anyone else. People passing by, taking night walks on the beach. Did we look our age to them? I remember being ten and watching my cousin, a stockbroker in his mid-twenties. He was formidable, intent on his life and career. Somehow, I expected twenty-three, when it came, to feel as old as my cousin looked. Perhaps I will feel older after graduate school. But I don't think age means anything once you get to the point where a little kid sees you as a grown-up. Once you're not little then you're big. How does eighty feel?

Miles waved a french fry in front of my lips and then waved it away again when it looked like I might bite.

'Eat, drink, and be jovial,' he said. 'Your food is getting cold and we all want to swim.'

I had bluefish, which can be a dark and greasy dining experience. The Grey Gull, however, bought their bluefish from the fishermen who pulled blues out of the Chesapeake Bay every afternoon. Tonight my portion carried a light cornflake coating and it had been pan-fried. Bluefish at its fresh best. Miles was right; my food was getting cold. I ate quickly, and he helped himself, as usual, to whatever it looked like I couldn't eat. This bothered my parents when I first took Miles home for the weekend; they wondered if I was getting enough sustenance. Because four years have passed and I have yet to look appreciably thinner, my parents have ceased to worry.

Surprisingly, Miles still manages to fit into his suits. He is the only one of us to do white collar work, because he is the only one of us who will apply to business school. Miles aims for Dartmouth's Amos Tuck School, and they expect two years of blood, sweat, and business before Miles can even think of applying. So Miles spends his days analyzing troubled companies for a consultant firm. He delves into accounts, speaks to employees, and writes out concise reports. Because he never trusts anything he can't prove, Miles is frighteningly good at this.

I often think that a writer could model a finicky

super-detective after Miles. He has a three-point dictum which he uses to evaluate companies, and I can imagine someone like Hercule Poirot expounding on the same sort of ideas, and applying them to crime. Miles' business creed and his life creed are one and the same. The creed revolves around variables, point of view, and sense of proportion. Nathan once demanded an explanation from Miles, because he said it all sounded very nice, but did Miles know what Miles meant by all that? Miles explained while looking out over the small spectacles which Katherine says give his face 'weight and balance'.

'I go to a company and see a manager first and listen to him. I nod a lot while he talks. Then I speak to an employee. Staff often have good ideas which they won't feel comfortable pointing out to a manager. This is point of view. Sense of proportion refers to the market that the company is trying to reach, also to how the company views itself in relation to competitors. The variables are things I don't know. The changes in interest rates, the amount of debt the company can carry, the demand for the company's product. I don't do miracles. I can't design a new product for a company that only produced one fad, say disco-dancing daisies.'

Miles brought back a 'disco-dancing daisy' from his visit to a diseased company called Psychedelic Botany. The dancing daisy was a plastic flower in a plastic pot which shook its plastic self all over when we played music. For weeks after the arrival of Miles' fantastic flora, our enraptured house cat watched unceasingly.

I contemplated Miles' suits while he finished my bluefish.

Beside me, Katherine stretched and yawned. 'Now', she said, 'we need to wait at least thirty minutes before we go into the water.' Nathan mouthed the words along with her. Because the two of them try to picnic on the beach whenever they eat together, Nathan hears those words like a refrain. I have heard them as well.

Marjorie sighed audibly. 'Katherine, try meditation – perhaps Zen.'

'I know, Marjorie, that you only suggest that as some kind of homeopathic tranquillizer. Spare me your snake oil. Seriously, you all have me to thank that you are not dying of cramps out in the waves,' Katherine said. 'But I certainly don't expect gratitude,' she added, aiming her comment at Miles particularly. Drawing in a breath, Miles geared up for his reply. I stuck a french fry in his mouth instead, because the deepening darkness of the sky accorded with calm.

Underneath us the sand had grown cool. Lights from a nearby dock and a full moon gave the water's surface an opaque sheen. The waves had calmed down to mere ripples.

'"But such a tide as moving seems asleep . . ."' said Nathan, who had delighted Marjorie by borrowing her first edition Tennyson collection. He poked me. 'Do you still entertain notions of entering law school? I imagine if and when the time comes, you might prefer "Crossing the Bar" to taking the Bar exam.'

'Oh God,' said Penman, looking distraught. 'Tennyson again. Please don't quote us that poetic birth defect, he was a pathetic sentimentalist.'

I looked past Penman and answered Nathan. 'I can't even imagine academia right now, give me a break.' Law school, which I had not decided with certainty to attend, seemed impossibly distant from this beach with my friends.

'Time's up,' said Miles as the small alarm on his watch went off. 'Thirty minutes exactly.'

On the wet sand sparks of phosphorescence flinted off our ankles and followed in our wakes when we whipped our feet through the water. Using his arms to churn the sea, Penman made whirlpools and watched the glow he created with a bemused expression. He doesn't come to the water during the day, partly because his skin is so pale that the sun gives him red welts, and partly because he keeps a peculiar schedule which seldom includes the hours before cocktails. Tiring of phosphorescence, Penman called to us that he was heading back to the house to watch a movie.

'It's a Neil Simon night. Perhaps a *Murder By Death* night. And after that, it might be a Kubrick night. Something grim.' Penman cackled, contemplating a late night spent as he liked best.

Except for Marjorie, we would all fade shortly after midnight. Marjorie doesn't sleep as far as we can tell, except for short, two or three minute naps which can happen at any time. As I remember from an early biology class, baby chickens do the same thing. They scuttle and chirp for a while, then, all of a sudden, the hairy heads bob and are still for about a minute. Just as suddenly, all is peep and totter again. I told this to Marjorie once, and she said it was very possible that she and the chicks shared the same biochemistry.

'My fowl biochemistry,' she had said, smiling minimally. 'It doesn't surprise me that it's you who draws that comparison. That's what you do, how you relate to everything.' Though I had pressed her to explain, she merely shrugged.

Back at the house we watched *Murder by Death* and cracked pistachios. Penman explained all the careful satire and informed us of when we should be laughing. At midnight we swept the shells from our laps, and Katherine and Nathan and Miles and I all went to bed. We left Marjorie to her chicken naps and Penman to his screen.

The next morning as Miles and I got ready for work, we heard groaning from a sofa in the corner of the kitchen. Miles left off playing with his beloved coffee maker, a contraption which uses a flat metal disc to bulldoze grounds out of the coffee.

'Penman, is that you?'

The sofa's groan came louder and Miles went over to inquire if Mr Bluebird was on Penman's shoulder, if everything was true, actual, and satisfactual. Penman cursed and sat up. 'I was attempting to sleep,' he said, flailing his arms in the air.

'Hard to do in the kitchen. The rest of us rise and shine,' said Miles. Miles wasn't looking very shiny. I knew he was in a foul mood because he would've liked to be asleep as well. Penman scowled at the world in general and went upstairs to the tiny closet in which he sleeps.

Finding a house to fit us all had comprised the second most difficult part of our group undertaking. Deciding where to go was the first hurdle. We explored many options, chiefly international, until we got a hint of how difficult it would be to obtain legal year-long work permits. Our thoughts back in the States again, we examined the West Coast. Coast was a common denominator in all our thoughts; East or West was the choice. Though the West Coast had the seductive lure known to anyone who has ever listened to the Beach Boys, we finally chose the East Coast for economic reasons. Not only did travelling costs add up more slowly, but for the same money, roughly about $200 a month from each of us, we thought we could get a four-bedroom house versus the one-bedroom California groove pad.

At an organizational powwow one night before graduation, we assembled in my small room to spread out a map and choose where to go. The weather was hot and my room was crowded; our gas station map of the East Coast diminished the floor space so that Nathan was practically straddling the fronds of my prized but unfruitful clementine tree. Katherine and Penman perched on my loft, and Marjorie and Miles shared the desk. I stood by the refrigerator and moderated the discussion. Miles wished to go to Maine. Katherine liked that but brandished Boston as the better option.

'Boston, Massachusetts,' murmured Marjorie. 'I've always suspected, Katherine, that you are a Yankee at heart.' The subtle words represented Marjorie's ultimate insult.

Nathan objected violently to the cold and muttered something about Florida. Marjorie favoured Wrightsville Beach, North Carolina because of a childhood summer spent thereabouts. Penman adored Palm Beach.

Somehow, we settled on Virginia Beach. Actually, 'somehow' is too vague a term. We finally decided on Virginia Beach because a man named Teddy Grunding, whom my father knew slightly, offered us all jobs there in a restaurant he was opening. Though this offer settled the question for us, by the time we got to Virginia Beach Mr Grunding was in jail, indicted for charges of gambling at his nightclub, a dubious hole on the waterfront called Where the Buoys Are. Penman was furious. I don't know which he thought more criminal, Mr Grunding's activities, or the pun in the name of his nightclub. Anyway, by then it was too late. Miles had found a terribly serious job not far from Virginia Beach, and we had settled the matter of a house.

Mr Grunding, when asked about where to live in Virginia Beach, had suggested we try his brother, Willy Grunding, and his Beachside Real Estate. On contacting Willy Grunding, however, the reply was brusque; they did not do rentals, they said. We tried five other agencies who all said they wouldn't handle rentals. After our first few tries, I stopped saying that we were six graduate students needing a house to rent; still, no one was interested. We decided to run an ad in the *Tidewater Tribune*. Keeping it simple, we wrote:

Large house needed for year-long lease. Furnished or Unfurnished; close to beach. $1,000 per month firm. August 1990–91. Reply: P.O. Box 100 c/o *Tidewater Tribune*.

We each contributed twenty dollars to run the ad for a month. In reply we received four letters. One came from Willy Grunding's real estate agency, and they wanted to know if we had anything to sell before we rented. A dirty envelope inscribed by crayon arrived from an elderly hippie who wanted to know if we might have a room where he could mellow out. The other two responses were houses for us to investigate.

John Hamden's was our first legitimate reply, and he gave us our first view of the Virginia Beach home. A bachelor professor at Old Dominion University, he had a year-long sabbatical leave in the offing. On the initial visit just Miles and I went to see the house. Winding our way through a neighbourhood of old cars and sandy streets, we found the water and John Hamden's place at nearly the same time.

It was a big cottage, with a long wide porch and open windows whose curtains fluttered at us like old ladies' hankies. John Hamden sat on his porch, waiting, with an enormous black cat between his feet.

'The cat's name is Odious,' he said, 'Dius for short. I'm John Hamden.'

His hair and his face and his shirt were rumpled. They all looked sun-dried. Small glasses sat on his head and old tennis shoes curled around his feet. In a gratifying way, he suited his house. The porch had a worn, slatted wood floor and a railing all around. The railing posts were smooth in places, and splintered in others where cats had sharpened generations of claws. In one corner a basket swing moved gently, and a bench occupied the wall next to it. We followed John Hamden inside.

'The house was designed by my grandmother and built by my grandfather. That was seventy years ago and it holds up all right. I have three bedrooms, two bathrooms and an attic with beds and not much insulation. You said you want to live here year-round?' He turned to face us as he spoke the last sentence, and a tiny piece of spittle whirled round with his head. My Dad and my dog both do that, usually when they are excited.

Miles answered Hamden's question with a nod, once down and twice up. 'There are six of us,' Miles said. 'We are about to be graduate students, but we are taking a year's rest first. You'd be able to meet us all, Sir.' I realized from Miles' tone that he really liked the house and was already worried that the man might not like or trust so much 'youth' here.

'What can you pay?'

'As we said in the ad,' said Miles, 'we can do up to $1,000 a month. I know that's not as much as you could normally get for the summer, and way over what you would usually get for the winter. We would take good care of the house.'

John Hamden looked at us for many moments. Silence didn't seem to bother him. People are understandably nervous about renting their houses out to large groups of humanity. Especially large young groups of humanity. He didn't look nervous, however. Just thoughtful.

'Do you mind ghosts?' he asked.

'What?'

Watching the expressions on our faces, John Hamden began to laugh. 'People expect them here, in a weather-beaten house in the proverbial Graveyard of the Atlantic. I don't have any, though. Kind of wish I did.' Still laughing, he extended a hand to Miles and then to me. He had offered us a year in his domain.

After thanking him we arranged a time the next week for all of us to meet. He asked us to dinner. Penman and Marjorie live in Richmond, and Katherine and Nathan come from Atlanta and Savannah respectively. They had all made it very clear that they would come any distance to view our prospective home. Before we signed a contract our decision had to be unanimous.

Though I was fairly certain everyone would like John Hamden's ancestral cottage, we still went to see the other house dredged up by our newspaper ad. The memory of that visit is one I cherish. Our other prospect was set in an estuary about fifteen miles from Virginia Beach proper. A long driveway led back through two brick columns at the side of the road. The columns proclaimed the name Singing Pines, and an oxidized copper beaver sat on top of each brick tower. I remember Miles and I looked at each other and raised eyebrows. My Nova did little credit to this entrance; this was the kind of driveway up which vintage Bentleys swept. Nevertheless, up we went.

The house itself would have been breathtaking if we were slightly myopic. It was a Civil War Southern mansion in rotten repair, and it made me think of Tara after the fall. We got out of the car and just stared. Square pillars, like ragged tributes to the most decadent Roman craftsmen, lifted a roof over the whole of the front porch. The roof dripped slate. Windows with jagged holes and multiple mullions gawked back at us.

After just moments, the mosquitoes whined their way onto our bare skin, and we started slapping. We slapped arms and legs and the backs of each other's necks and each dead mosquito left a tiny smear of blood. Running for the front door, I tripped on a brick and sprawled ungracefully.

A voice called from an upper window to ask if one of us was Miles; he had set up the appointment. Miles yelled that yes, he was indeed Miles and could we come in? A few minutes later the front door opened to reveal a woman between the ages of eighty and one hundred. She wore a skirted bathing suit, the kind with a built-in chest, and running shoes. Her sparse hair showed patches of scalp, and she was either very deeply tanned or black.

'I've been swimming and I was just going to change

when you happened up. Bad fall there, young lady. Probably needs a stitch. My grandson fell there in '69 and ripped up his leg so bad he needed a skin graft. Care for some iced tea? I make it myself and none of that powdered stuff that clumps up in the humidity. We won't sit on the porch. Damn mosquitoes chew on every uncovered bit of you. Like the house?'

She took us inside through a hallway which appeared to bisect the building. We went all the way back through the house and out to a screened porch on the back side. Every board we toed creaked under our weight and I felt a need to step gingerly. Peeling paint banked the edges of the floor, which was lovely old wood worn smooth; the timbers were actually gullied in the middle, where years of feet had walked.

'I'm Alice Rose Cromwell, one of the Charleston Cromwell's, and a Birmingham Rose. I am just dying to get out of this heap and do some touring. But I can't leave Singing Pines alone for a second and I need some renters. You could have it free if you were a handyman and willing to do a bit of work.'

Free. Miles' ears perked up. His Scottish ancestors would be proud. Not only does Miles make friends with every bill in his wallet, *free* has a personal religious meaning to him. At the time I was worried, because though the house had charm and character, a nice fiesty old landlady, and probably fifty genteel phantoms, it looked as habitable as a turtle shell.

After Miles asked if we could view the rooms, Alice Rose Cromwell took us on a wander which exposed a massive house of great staircases and high ceilings. A bedroom which we saw on the top floor had, in one corner, a heap of wood and plaster which turned out to be part of the roof. Birds were coming in through the resultant hole. Alice Rose Cromwell said the house was well ventilated. Probably the city council didn't condemn it out of respect for the Cromwell family.

Miles looked daunted by the time we got through the second floor, and I was grateful for that. Miss Cromwell asked us what we thought. Miles and I looked desperately at one another, and then I began to speak, slowly and carefully.

'Well, Miss Cromwell, this looks like a very fine home. It also looks like a very delicate home, and we are six large people who are very active. I just don't know that we would be the best tenants for a house like this.'

She interrupted me. 'What you are busy tryin' not to say is that this heap of dung might fall down on you and you're a little worried. I can understand that. Take a house nearby then, and come and see me when you're in town. Now, care for a refill on that tea?'

After promising to visit her, we departed. For me, the promise to see her again was no social nicety. I yearned to return and bring Marjorie along with me. Though I felt sure she would be glad that Miles and I had ruled out living at Singing Pines, I expected Marjorie and Miss Alice Rose to get on like grits and gravy. As two Southern Belles who had travelled roads less taken, they had much in common. And I wished to be present when their paths merged for a time; indeed, I planned to engineer the meeting.

* * *

On the evening of Tuesday, June the twelfth, we all convened for the first time at John Hamden's beach house. When we arrived he told us that we would be celebrating the birthday of Queen Elizabeth II of England, since only the day before her birthday had been celebrated in Australia.

'Just practising,' he said. 'I'll be doing my sabbatical in Sydney.'

We started with Castlemaine beer, Stilton and water crackers. While John Hamden chatted downstairs with Penman, Nathan, and Miles, Katherine, Marjorie and I prowled the house and staked out rooms. We weren't exactly sure who would be sharing rooms at that point, but we figured we could put our claims in anyway.

Of the three bedrooms upstairs, two faced the water and were small. The other bedroom was double the size of the first two put together, and it had a small sitting area in the corner. John obviously used this room, for his books were everywhere, and a small computer nested on a desk near the bed. It was on, and the flashing indicator displayed a page stopped in mid-sentence. Marjorie drifted toward it, then halted in front of a bookstand to finger a worn copy of Kierkegaard's *A Sickness Unto Death*. Katherine and I headed up one more flight of stairs to the attic.

The attic was a long low room panelled in pine. Two dormer windows looked out front to the street, and three looked out back to the sea. An old four-poster bed without a canopy sat in between the two front windows, which were full of a fan each. The bed seemed a good vantage point from which to admire the room, so we sat on it.

'What do you think of it?' I asked Katherine, feeling responsible for the cottage and hoping she'd like it. I knew the answer would be painful, but I was helpless not to ask her. Katherine can always find something wrong, but I am pathetically optimistic. The potential satisfaction of pleasing someone who cannot easily be pleased tantalizes me. Seeking her approval is hugely masochistic, and I am usually annoyed with myself for trying.

'It's not bad, but then, we haven't lived in it yet. I can't really tell.' She probably would be more negative about the palace of Versailles. Absurdly, I was pleased.

Watching her reconnoitre the attic room, however, I had to curb a growing irritation. Katherine examined the four walls and everything in between as though the room would be hers and Nathan's. Perhaps because I had seen the house first, I had assumed the right to choose Miles' and my room. Katherine's usual badgering, I decided, would not make me give up this attic for her. Like the slow swelling of a soufflé, I puffed with indignation. And all before Katherine and I had exchanged even one word about allocating bedrooms.

Marjorie's head rose out of the stairway, and, after a quick peer about, she came to join us. 'So, this is the room we'll all fight about.' Marjorie was good at picking up on quiet tensions. 'Let's give it to whoever gets up first. Then we can all use it the rest of the day without bothering anyone.' We plucked at the knobbly chenille knots which made up the soft pattern of the bedspread.

'I think we should all live up here.' As the earliest riser, I felt generous. Katherine vetoed my suggestion, saying shortly that Nathan snored. Marjorie volunteered that Penman could lift the bed linens with his horrific gas.

'How do you know?' asked Katherine casually. Too casually. I laughed inside as I realized that Katherine thought she had discovered a sexual aspect to the Penman/Marjorie relationship. She feared her hypothesis on homosexual leanings would have to be radically altered. Oh, angst.

Marjorie fixed her eyes effortlessly on Katherine. 'Sometimes Penman spends the night at my house when we've been up late. The cat who always sleeps in his guest room comes to sleep with me because Penman makes the atmosphere unpleasant. Naturally, I myself have never experienced the air in Penman's guest bedroom, but the source of the unpleasantness is loud enough to penetrate my wall.' Marjorie widened her eyes to look dewy and innocent, and I almost laughed aloud. Stupidly, when I first met Marjorie, I thought she had no sense of humour.

Six different degrees of humour – some farther advanced than others along the evolutionary ladder of laughter, allow Nathan, Katherine, Marjorie, Penman, Miles, and me to mingle our lives the way we do. Up in the attic I had my first notion that living together, as opposed to seeing each other every day, might require more than humour. The link between Katherine and Marjorie is fragile, and best strengthened by the absence of one from the other. Thoughtfully, I followed my friends down the attic stairs, then the main stairs. We detoured to take a look at the second-floor bathroom.

In the manner of someone carrying out recent instructions about what to examine in houses, Katherine checked the water pressure on the taps and then flushed the toilet. 'It's vital that the plumbing works properly. With six of us, things could become unhygienic quickly.' Katherine's mouth had a pursed look that showed me how she'd look when she was ninety. She leaned over to watch the swirl of water empty and refill, and then she pronounced the toilet a good one. I knew better than to comment. Marjorie, however, reached over to pat a confidential hand on Katherine's arm.

'I'm sure that commode came from a good family.'

Ignoring her, Katherine went to the stairs. We followed the smell of a barbecue grill. I guess that feelings of *déjà vu* for the future are more accurately called premonitions, but as we went downstairs I remember that I had definite visions, so real that they might already have happened, of our future in that house. I remember being sure the house would often smell of food cooked outdoors. But few of our meals in the year ahead could rival the dinner John Hamden gave us that night.

On the grill lay large pieces of salmon which had been rubbed all over with mayonnaise, then basted with lemon, butter and dill. The fire had applewood chips to give the fish extra flavour. Because the applewood bits had been moistened before going to the flames, the grill issued forth clouds of smoke which filled the back patio. Defined by flagstones and contained by a stone wall, the space was about twelve foot square. Huge bundles of sea grass waved just outside the stone wall, and, over a small rise, we could hear the sea.

'Have you ever had trouble with rising water?' Nathan asked, his nostrils quivering. The smell of our imminent meal filled the air, the smoke richly exotic and freshly fishy. The aroma sounded a sensual dinner gong.

'Occasionally a hurricane will whip things up to the point where I get worried, but the water hasn't reached up here in my lifetime. Wind has taken the roof off and broken glass, but I imagine the place needs a bit of refurbishment now and again anyhow. You may be cold here in the winter, particularly in that attic. The weather will probably stay warm all the way into the middle of November, but the wind will be chilly and raw after that, maybe before as well. The main thing is that it's unpredictable. One Halloween it was so hot that little kids wore their bathing suits as costumes. The ones who didn't, though, got some extra sympathy candy from me.' John Hamden grinned as he said that, and I thought suddenly that he would have made a good father.

'I think if you all would give me a hand with some things in the house, we should be ready to eat,' John said. So we brought out red-skin potato salad and a plate of tomatoes and a pitcher of tea. Along with the plates and cutlery there was a basket covered with a linen napkin.

'Perhaps he fashioned these himself.' We were in the kitchen, where Penman was rooting under the napkin at some small puffy bread rolls in the basket. John Hamden, who overheard him, explained.

'I'd like to say I made them myself, but it is a neighbour, Mrs Ciucci, who bakes those for me. They are called *ciabatta*, an Italian mix of flour and olive oil. She made lots for us tonight, but I guarantee there won't be any left.'

Penman reached for one and bit, and his face lit with pleasure. 'Toothsome,' he said, wiping his mouth meticulously.

We filled our plates on the patio and then went out to the dunes to eat. Napped with a sauce of cucumber and dill, the salmon was pink and tender. The potato salad, with its spicy vinaigrette and red and green peppers, complemented the fish blissfully. And, after sampling the sliced tomatoes – dripping as they were with extra-virgin olive oil, freshly ground pepper, and the occasional chunky morsel of sea salt – Miles returned to the patio and brought out the entire bowl of them.

With closed eyes Penman savoured a slice of tomato, making small 'ummmm' noises which surely would have incurred the despair of Lila, housekeeper and arbiter of manners at his grand Richmond home. Aloud, Penman wondered whether such gastronomic wonders came from Hanover County, source of famed Virginia tomatoes.

'Except', said Penman, chewing slowly and with great deliberation, 'there's a sort of zest and piquancy which Hanover tomatoes don't usually achieve.'

'Penman, you will someday make a fine and pompous wine lover,' said Nathan.

John Hamden kindly killed off the tomato snobbery. 'The flavour over which you are mulling, Penman, is a direct result of our Virginia Beach earth. The "piquancy" comes from the fish bits used faithfully by cottage gardeners to fertilize crops. Our fields smell truly aromatic on hot days.'

For dessert we had a Pavlova, a round meringue base spread with a layer of sweetened cream, then a layer of strawberries arranged on top. According to John Hamden, the dessert was an Australian favourite.

'Cheers to Queen Elizabeth,' he said.

'This has truly been a feast of fat things,' Katherine observed. 'Thank you very much. After that dessert my arteries may not recover for a week, but it was worth it.'

'Actually', said John Hamden, 'the only fatty bits were in the cream. Meringue is nothing more than egg whites and sugar.' The skin around his eyes began to crinkle, but his tone was serious as he said, 'a colleague of mine is doing research on cholesterol free eggs. Depending on how quickly he works, the market may soon be flooded with hens' eggs containing no cholesterol and reduced fat.'

'How bizarre,' I thought for a moment. 'Katherine, wouldn't you be thrilled if those eggs grew up to be fat-free chickens?'

'I don't think it works that way,' Katherine said. But she smiled in my direction.

We all made contented and grateful noises about dinner. John Hamden said it was a pleasure; he was curious to know the people who would be living in his home. After stretching luxuriously he suggested we head inside and talk the words of business that were necessary.

Kitchens in general are very relaxed places to talk of serious matters, and John Hamden's kitchen was a particularly relaxed place. The walls and ceiling were painted yellow. Rag rugs mushroomed on various parts of the pine floor, and blue curtains fell on the windows. The appliances were good, but old. Only a new microwave sitting by the refrigerator announced modern comfort. The great surprise, though, was a large blue Aga stove which dominated the whole wall of counter space. Katherine and I first approached it with awed expressions. John Hamden watched us, very amused.

'Those aren't quite what people build them up to be, you know. The actual interior baking space doesn't permit very even air circulation. It makes the whole kitchen very warm, though, and I'm quite fond of it. Its name is Bucephalus. Originally, my grandmother had a wood-burning Aga in this kitchen, one she brought with her from Sweden. Three years ago I got fed up with carrying wood, and so I bought this one. Grandmother called hers Achilles.

'The stove represents about the only thing of value in the house. I have a computer upstairs which I will take with me, but everything else stays for you to use. Normally, I think the renter asks for a security deposit. Having met you all, I don't think that's necessary. I think the best security is that you like the house, and I can tell you do.' I remember that he smiled at us when he said that, and we all smiled back, liking him.

We did the dishes while we talked. Eventually, Miles

and John had sat down to write a contract for the house. Running from August the first, to August the first of the following year, the rent would be $800 a month. We would be responsible for all utilities, and in periods interrupted by our arrivals and departures, the bills would be prorated. On finishing the impromptu document, we all signed and Miles wrote a cheque for the first month's rent. Only after we had moved in and begun to receive the local newspapers did we realize what a kindness John Hamden had done us. Houses far shabbier than ours rented for $800 *per week* during the months of June to September. We figured that something other than money motivated John Hamden.

Early on the morning of August the first, Miles and I arrived to take up residence at the beach. John Hamden had to leave for the airport by eight-thirty a.m., and as we figured we needed to ask for instructions on water pipes and heating, we arrived at seven. After we had helped John to get his baggage moved into the mini-van he had rented at the Norfolk International Airport, we ate a mobile muesli breakfast as John moved around the house and explained last minute details. Had Katherine been there, she would have been keying in his instructions on her laptop computer; as it was I had to take a few notes. We finished up back in the kitchen where John informed us that he had been able to dredge up a ghost for us.

'On dark typhoon-filled evenings, a shade known as "The Captain" comes to warn residents of Chicks Cove Beach to get out before it's too late. Legend has it the

Captain wears a great grey cape and a black watch cap. Those who have seen him say that where his eyes should be is . . . nothing. Supposedly, he's the spirit of a North Carolina merchant skipper whose boat went down with all hands during a storm some time last century. He drowned about two miles offshore here, and there is a wreck that divers go down to see, but I think that's from World War I. At any rate, be alert for two knocks on the back door during a storm. He never goes to a front door, only the back, and only when the back door opens out on the water side. He also won't warn tourists – only residents.' John Hamden's eyes got very small as laughter wrinkles swallowed up his face.

'Even if the rest of the story wasn't embellished by locals, that last bit certainly contains some of the prejudice felt against "summer people". I think the Captain, having been a trader in his earthly years, would be a good phantom capitalist. The tourists bring in a lot of money.'

We thanked him for our ghost and for the sets of keys he gave us. He'd had six sets cut and had attached each set to a key ring with a tiny plastic shark on it.

'G'day,' he said and shook our hands and wished us well. We waved goodbye to him as his mini-van manoeuvered slowly down the driveway and away.

'Let's get settled before anyone else gets here.' Miles' tone was mean. We'd spent the night before at my home in Washington D.C. In order to arrive in Virginia Beach by seven this morning, we had left my house at four a.m. Arising before nine a.m. irritates Miles fiercely. Not surprisingly, his wrath at having to drive before the sun climbed even to visibility was tumultuous. Miles had dealt with his anger by pouring it into his foot, which then pressed hard on the accelerator.

After nearly running down an old MG that wouldn't get out of the fast lane, Miles had swerved our car around the MG so fast that I had to stifle a shriek and a fragrant expletive. Normally, he might have apologized. Since he was tired and grumpy, however, he had merely looked annoyed at my cowardice.

Miles always drives in a carefully maniacal fashion. Though that sounds like an oxymoron, it's not. He has the skills to be an excellent driver, but he hates being in the car and so goes as quickly as possible. He's very aggressive about the fast lane. Contrary to his view of my cowardice, I've had the chance to develop great courage over the years as I've sat in the passenger seat next to him. I've also had a chance to learn that when Miles and I drive together, our most harmonious positions are me behind the wheel, and Miles stretched horizontally on a fully reclining passenger seat.

'How do you feel about living in the same house – the same room, actually – with me?' I had put the question to Miles as we blasted through the early morning on our drive down from Washington.

'I can't hear a word,' said Miles. After saying that fresh air helped him remain awake, he had opened all the car windows. An airy roar surrounded us. Even after I spoke, Miles made no move to raise any windows; he scowled at me as I rolled mine up.

'Co-habitating differs wildly from co-existing, Miles!' The noise was such that I still had to shout in his ear. 'I am concerned about living with you! In four years we have never lived together, and it will be odd to share everything!'

Miles turned his head to look at me in pure disgust; the car seized the moment to swerve in tandem with his head, then straightened as Miles looked forward again. 'This is a fine time to raise that concern!' he said.

'Roll up your windows, Miles! I promise you won't go to sleep. Honestly, are you at all worried about living with me?'

Shaking his head, Miles raised the windows partway. 'Of course I'm not worried about living with you. What have we done in the past four years, huh? Though you didn't live in my room technically, or I in yours, we might as well have. So what's the big deal? You've used my toothbrush, worn my clothes, we share a bank account, and I've seen you pee.'

'Disgusting. And we don't "share a bank account". We set up a joint account with both of our savings in it, because you said that way we move into a band of higher interest. The arrangement does not mean that your money is my money or vice versa. And I'm not saying that I want it to be!

'All I mean, Miles, is that what we will be doing in the coming year resembles, in essence, being married. And we are not.'

'So what? We have agreed, on the fortunately infrequent times when we have discussed it, that marriage waits until we know what we want to do with our lives, and whether we can do it together.'

'Fine.' My feelings were hurt the first time he said that, and they weren't appreciably less bruised this time. Miles looked straight ahead and kept silent, though as we neared the beach house he patted my knee. And after a moment I patted his.

During our silent drive I had time to reflect on why Miles and I don't discuss futures. In fact, I realized, not any of the six of us discuss futures. It is a tacit agreement – almost an unbroken rule – one which other people find strange but which we arrived at without debate. The friendship between us all is a rare thing, like a perfect menu with Katherine and Miles acting as two citrus sorbets which scour the palate in between courses. In the future lie normal life events which will disrupt the friendships between the six of us. Even though disruption may strengthen the friendships which survive, for the moment we don't talk about that. Futures are taboo, and present is perfect.

The absolute immediate present, however, looked of dubious perfection; Miles still suffered from morning grumps. As we moved out to the car in preparation for unloading, I realized that I *walked*, and Miles *stalked*.

'The Captain will come and get you if you don't watch out,' I informed him positively, knowing that reason isn't always the best tool for tempering his ire. I have long thought that awe-inspiring anger on my part might be an interesting way to counter Miles' temper. Theatrical anger, however, looks best when the angry party possesses statuesque proportions and a long slender neck so that the head can waggle back and forth with the force of one's words. I am tall and thin, with a thick neck and an elastic sort of face with more smile lines than I ought to have at twenty three. Anger just doesn't suit me.

Anger looked pretty silly on Miles, too. It was just

after nine a.m., and we were finally at the beach, and he was, all in all, quite pleased with his present existence. Graciously, he handed me a bulky bag of sports equipment with which to lumber into the house.

As we had all decided way back in June, he and I took the attic room. We got it by a process of grudging elimination. Nathan had been put off by the lack of insulation and the promise of cold mornings. Since Katherine slept with Nathan, that ruled her out as well, though she was not happy about it. Marjorie had said she wanted to be able to visit the attic frequently, but she didn't want to have to clean it. Saying that she would only dirty as large a space as belonged to her, Marjorie claimed one of the small back bedrooms with a view of the sea. Penman had wanted the attic badly, but not badly enough to alter his sleeping habits; we all wanted to be able to use the room before late afternoon. So it was up two flights of stairs to the attic that Miles and I carried our baggage.

On that first August day at the beach, the morning sun filled our long low room and promised a day hot like hellfire. Despite the earliness of the morning, the breeze from the fan already felt necessary. When the last suitcase reached the attic, we collapsed on a sofa fitted into the far wall and watched the water.

'Do you remember what time the tides are?' Miles asked. Quickly and excitedly we had eyeballed a tide chart stuck by a magnet to the refrigerator door.

'I think high tide is at two-thirty p.m. and low at eight-thirty this evening, but I may have the wrong month.' I couldn't remember if we had examined the first of July, or August.

'The water seems pretty high for not nearly high tide,' he said, pointing at a line of seaweed and sticks which seemed to indicate the highest water mark. 'Do you think local laws allow for bonfires on the beach?'

I didn't answer him; I was listening carefully to what sounded like a car pulling up. Then another. Then Penman's voice, loudly. 'God it's hot. Sensible people sleep through the parts of the day which encourage skin to blister. Marjorie, did you say this charming retreat has no air-conditioning? How quaint. I shall investigate the possibilities of having the whole house refrigerated. Do we have John Hamden's number in Sydney?'

'Penman, you inveterate crank, come feel the breeze,' called Miles, trying to throw his voice up and out the front window. The fan blades chopped through Miles' words, and Marjorie and Penman heard only a muffled shout. We waited for them to come up to the attic, and they did. That's how our year together began.

3

By the end of August, we had survived together for nearly a month. I'm certain that living together, all of a sudden, with five other people, is more difficult than marriage. Instead of one person's foibles, peccadilloes, and peculiar moods, you get six. My family at home has six people in it. But we all have to love each other. My mother *insists*. Families have different bonds than friends do; bonds that might not be as strong as friendship's bonds, but bonds that are more secure and consistent, based on birth and blood. Summer camp, where people live together in little tents, with groups of four to six bodies, always works best with young kids. Little kids have more of a collective personality, I think. Little kids seldom have identity crises, simply because they haven't had a chance to develop personalities and become possessive about them. They have character but they aren't yet characters. Characters are very hard to live with. In our own ways, all of us at the house in Virginia Beach could be labelled 'characters'. It might have been easier to live with little kids.

Penman and Marjorie come from huge houses with lots of space. They have never picked up after themselves because their families have people who 'do' for them. Penman often told us stories of Lila, an elderly woman who took care of him when he was wee, and who made him caramel poundcake and fried chicken to bring back to his college dormroom. When I met Lila last summer, I was out on Penman's veranda eating a bowl of mint chip ice-cream with a silver spoon. Lila chastised me gently for not using a silver ice-cream fork.

'All these bits of silver have their own purpose, honey, and someone's got to be left in this day and age to know what to use them for,' she twittered. Leading me back into the luxurious cool of Penman's home, Lila ushered me into the pantry. Here reposed the silver flatware in its infinitude and exceptional variety. Lila introduced me to the silver cake-crumb scrapers, the relish servers, and the berry spoons, just in case I might ever need them. Only the week before, Lila said, she had caught Penman's younger brother using a slotted silver chutney ladle to scoop out his kitten's litter box. She worried for the family, she told me. I remember trying to keep a straight face, which was easier than it might have been since most of my attention was on chasing my ice-cream around with my fork.

As for Marjorie, though we had never heard her discuss a favoured family retainer, she must have had some sort of help in looking after herself. I picked up her laundry once when she was ill and found that she dry cleaned her socks and under-wear because she didn't know how to use a washing machine.

Not surprisingly, neither Penman nor Marjorie had any concept of having to do dishes or clean a toilet or how to vacuum. Penman loved to cook, though. He had beautiful books detailing the production of beef medallions artistically placed on plates of swirled, multi-coloured cream sauces, and home-made wild mushroom pasta with prosciutto and carbonara sauce. His efforts were always grandiose and cheerful, but he did not think to clean up after himself. It took the rest of us a while to figure out that Penman's messes were the ones which stayed in the sink until we needed a particular bowl or plate he had used. Nathan had a long talk with Penman, and after that we decided to set down some house rules.

The house rules conclave was held out on the beach one morning in September. In deference to the occasion we wore shirts over our bathing suits. Katherine came with her notebook and Marjorie with her tea. We all brought righteously defensive attitudes. I suppose I have more insight now into the atmosphere at OPEC meetings. As the sun rose in the sky, the breeze stilled and biting flies added interest to the proceedings. Katherine started.

'Though we are all good friends, we will not con-tinue to be with the increasing number of domestic confrontations. If I could suggest a few ground rules. First, whatever mess each person makes, that person cleans up that mess no matter where or when.'

Nathan objected. 'Puppies make messes. People

don't. Let's just say that we need to show consideration for each other. I think we can approach this like adults.'

Miles looked angry, and his voice verged on a shout. 'Being adult doesn't get the toilet clean or the wastebaskets empty. I think we need some rules.' He glared from Katherine to me to Marjorie. Miles was particularly angry today because when he went to the bathroom for his morning ablutions he had discovered the remains of a feminine hygiene product in the toilet. The actual workings of the human body have always disgusted him. I think his mother, an OB-GYN, gave him too much detail at an early age. Miles can't stand blood or needles. When Nathan gives himself insulin shots, Miles has to leave the room.

'Yes,' said Penman. 'I think rules are necessary. Particularly regarding food.' He looked pointedly at me, and I looked out to examine a speck on the horizon. Just at that moment, a bit of tension existed between Penman and me.

At the core, I am a thoughtful person. My thoughtfulness skews slightly, however, when I come in contact with food; I have little will power about things I want to eat. Penman learned that last night when he got home from work two hours later than I did. On my arrival I was ravenous. After scouring the fridge I found a box of pizza with three tantalizing pieces inside. I ate two, then called a pizza place to deliver more. Since no one delivers pizza at two in the morning, I trekked off to our all-night grocery store, and, conscience-stricken, bought a huge Italian roll. I put the roll in the pizza box with a note of

apology and a promise of reparation, and then I went
to bed.

Penman, reported Marjorie this morning, had turned
puce with anger. She thought his ears had quivered, and
said his face had gotten all tight and bloated like he was
in a faulty decompression chamber. He cursed me and
my love of food and swore to seek retribution. He had
been looking forward to his leftover pizza all night.

'What was worse', Penman huffed at me face to face
as soon as I awoke, 'was that you had the unmitigated
gall to replace the pizza with a sandwich. Imagine
opening a pizza box to find a sandwich and one token
slice! Marjorie felt obligated to come upstairs with me
last night and barricade the attic steps so I couldn't
throttle you.'

'How terrifying,' said Miles. Penman's body has the
aerodynamics of a runner bean, and it is an effort,
occasionally, for Penman to lift a beer to his lips. 'At
least she sought a food from the same genre – Italian
pizza, Italian roll.' Miles did not quite understand the
situation. He knew I was sorry after the fact for having
taken Penman's food, and he knew I would supply
Penman with another pizza. He forgave me. The rest
of the house felt similarly.

'The mass of men are simply a snivelling lot without
pizza pies, Penman. You will live,' said Marjorie.

But I understood how Penman felt when he arrived
home to find the pizza gone. I had understood that even
while I drooled over his two pieces of pizza. My basic
human kindness had ended where my taste buds began.
That realization was a humiliating one, especially for
a fat child grown up slim. Had the situation been

reversed, I could have forgiven Penman. My own love of food would probably have helped me to empathize with his need for pizza. Obviously he didn't see it that way.

Back in our meeting, Nathan held up his hands for quiet. As his long hair spread over his shoulders and caught the sun, I thought suddenly of a prophet of domestic tranquillity. His next words caught me completely unprepared.

'I want everyone to dig a hole in the sand, a hole approximately the size of his or her own ass. It must be at least six inches deep, but you may stop earlier if you reach damp sand. Please dig.'

Charged with the novelty of the instructions, we made the sand fly. Nathan told us to sit in our holes.

'Now. Look about you. Look at the horizon, which is nearly six miles away. Look at fiddler crab holes. At small children losing their bathing suits in the waves. Hear the sea oats rustle. We are at the beach.' He was silent for a moment. 'Let's not fuck up a rare opportunity to enjoy being here by annoying each other. Chores do need to get done. I suggest one person each week be responsible for general maintenance, for getting everything into a state in which we all feel comfortable living.' Nathan forestalled any comment by waving his hands. 'If we all decide, right now, that that's how it's going to work, then that's it.'

No one said anything, and Nathan smiled on us beatifically. 'Psychologically', he said, 'sitting in a hole puts one in a far more humble and agreeable mood. Just think what great progress would be achieved if political assemblies could be held whilst conferees assumed the stance generally reserved for taking a shit.' Nathan leaned back on his elbows and closed his eyes. Katherine looked at him in reproof.

'Your word choice is straight from the gutter, Nathan. You know I object to that.'

'What do you propose for the ordering of our comestibles?'

'You mean food, don't you, Penman? Let's have a common fund, also a common shelf, for milk, orange juice, and bread. Then everyone gets part of a shelf in the refrigerator for their own use. It will work out,' Nathan said.

It all seemed very sensible to us. We sat in our holes for a while longer and had a chat.

'I've never used a vacuum cleaner before,' said Penman, looking perplexed.

'We'll look on it as a chance to expand our inner potential,' said Marjorie, who patted his shoulder and looked tolerant.

Miles asked Nathan how his new job at the Pizza Hut was going. Nathan was the last of us to find employment. I imagine his appearance was a considerable obstacle over which his prospective employer had to bound. Though his hair is always pulled back neatly, and though Katherine sometimes braids it and ties a bow, Nathan isn't what the classified ads termed 'well-presented'.

Nathan works all hours at the Pizza Hut. Overtime pays double, and his finances are always stretched. During college Nathan, who is very generous with money, tended not to have any left over for things like text books and board bills. Next fall he'll start medical school at The Medical College of Virginia on a full scholarship. Though he got into Stanford, he would never have been able to afford tuition, let alone eating or sleeping in Palo Alto.

At present, Nathan only needs to make enough money to pay his share of the rent and to support his periodical habit. The furniture in Katherine and Nathan's room consists of piles of magazines, tied with hempen slipknots for easy access to back issues. *The Economist,* complete back to 1984, serves as a stool. *Theology Today* and *National Geographic* dating from 1986 and 1980 respectively, serve as a nightstand. At least two dozen lesser-known periodicals, ranging in subject matter from a Joseph Conrad newsletter to a British magazine devoted solely to weapons, make up a sort of bench. Before we moved in, Nathan had all of his magazine subscriptions switched to our Virginia Beach address, so something interesting comes for him in every afternoon's mail bundle. In fact, marshalling the week's magazines neatly onto the coffee table would probably have to be one of the chores done by whoever managed the maintenance. It would not be gracious to complain about that task, though. We are all very busy reading Nathan's magazines.

Our cleaning conference cleared grievances over the house and left us to argue about other, more important things. Perhaps fear of being made to sit in the sand again kept our disagreements mainly agreeable. Usually, house strife concerned trivial matters. For instance, Miles and Katherine had a week-long tussle over what kind of milk our general fund would buy. Katherine preferred skimmed milk over Miles' choice of two per cent fat. Miles called her candidate 'blue milk' and said that lack of substance gave skimmed milk the same hue found in the papery skin of old people's hands. Katherine said fatty milk promoted heart disease. We listened to the half-witted skirmish until Penman asked if we could buy both kinds of milk.

'Two per cent fat for me to foam for my cappuccino, and skimmed milk with which to water my plants,' he said.

So every week we bought a gallon of each. My mother would say that obviously our lives had need of greater thrills if we could devote our attentions to conflicts so minuscule. Mothers are nearly always right. I doubted that for a while when I was growing up, but now I'm old enough to know it's true.

Amazingly wrinkled and brown, the face of Miss Alice Rose Cromwell contracted upwards with the force of her smile, the folds of her cheeks seeming to layer around her eyes. Her grin resembled nothing less than the raising of French blinds. In response I felt my own face pucker, and even Marjorie smiled perceptibly. An auspicious start, I thought, for the inaugural acquaintance between the two most interesting Southern Belles in my sphere of existence.

'Why, hello,' called Miss Alice Rose from her perch atop the nearest of Singing Pines' entry columns.

'Hello!' we called back, wondering at the sight of her.

Miss Alice Rose wore a cotton print dress and an enormous straw hat tied around her head with a white silk scarf – tail ends fluttering under her chin. As such she looked primed for the afternoon tea at which she had requested Marjorie and I join her. But instead of sitting, delicately ensconced, behind a fat silver teapot, Miss Alice Rose knelt on a ten-foot high brick column with her knees clamped around one of the two copper beavers which posted guard here at the entrance to her grand old home. Miss Alice Rose's hands were gloved – yellow rubber – and a bouquet of steel wool blossomed in one fist.

Waving the steel wool at us, she pointed to the subject of her labours. 'Seagull plop,' said Miss Alice Rose matter-of-factly, indicating the beaver's white wig. 'I just can't stand those birds. And I don't believe I had a violent bone in this body until now. It's taken well-nigh ninety years and a couple of fecund flying rats to make me yearn for a shotgun. Really', she said, thumping the beaver's chest affectionately, 'the gulls ought to have more respect for these old boys than to land on their heads and dump a mess of bodily refuse. The sun bakes the stuff, and it's terrible hard work to remove. I'll have to come back later with some acid.'

My car idled on the edge of the driveway as Miss Alice Rose spoke to us. Marjorie and I gaped back at her, craning our heads out the window. On me the mouth agape resembled an abyss; Marjorie's surprise showed in a pinhole-sized opening. 'She is an extraordinary woman,' pronounced Marjorie, hardly moving her lips at all. 'Do you think she flew up there?'

Miss Alice Rose knelt on that column and no visible ladder had aided her ascent. Giving the beaver's wig a final swipe, Miss Alice Rose called, 'just a minute longer, girls. I'll be right down.' Then she proceeded to shimmy down the square column, feet first, searching for tiny footholds in the crumbling pointwork between the bricks. Marjorie's eyebrows rose measurably.

'May we give you a lift up to the house?' I asked, and immediately Marjorie hopped out of the passenger seat and moved to the back of the car.

Miss Alice Rose peeled off her rubber gloves, depositing them and her wad of steel wool at the base of the brick column. 'Why yes, my dears. It's such a warm day, that would be lovely.'

'Miss Alice Rose, this is Marjorie,' I said as she settled herself in the front seat. 'Marjorie, Miss Alice Rose Cromwell.'

In the passing of the next sixty seconds I drove the length of Singing Pines' drive, and Miss Alice Rose and Marjorie completed their introductions. It took the two of them under a minute to determine both that Marjorie's mother played tennis every Thursday morning with the grandniece of Miss Alice Rose's childhood bosom friend and that Marjorie's father was the escort of choice at the debut of one of Miss Alice Rose's godchildren's daughters. Their conversation was the most expert version I'd yet heard of '*Who's yowah motha, who's yowah diddy*' – the high-born Southern word game used to deduce whether a new acquaintance's *people* were quality. From what I could tell, Miss Alice Rose Cromwell was not a traditional Belle. Nor was Marjorie, but in the South, one could disown one's breeding, but one would never be disowned by it. Marjorie and Miss Alice Rose played their parts as unconsciously as they did superbly.

'Well,' said Miss Alice Rose, beaming at Marjorie.

'It's a delight to meet you. Let's have some tea, shall we?'

She led us to a corner of her veranda where a table had been set with flowers. 'I'll just pop in and get the tea. Would you girls be so kind as to uncover the plates?' So saying, our hostess disappeared into the house.

'Haviland,' said Marjorie with satisfaction, turning over the back of a paper-thin porcelain plate and noting its label. 'And', she said, tapping the handle of a silver butter knife, 'Tiffany Faneuil with her family crest, very tasteful. My mother would positively moo with approval.'

'Good God, Marjorie. You sound like Penman.'

'My roots. Like them or lump them. Shall we uncover the plates?'

We did, and the prospects of tea as a repast grew more pleasurable with every plate. On a silver, three-tiered cake stand sat miniature pastries: *millefeuilles* the size of dominoes, strawberry tarts no bigger than doughnut holes, and éclairs like infants' pinkies. Off to the side, on a footed, kidney-shaped platter of heavy silver lay the sandwiches, piles of diminutive triangles with intriguing fillings.

'Hmmm', purred Marjorie, peeling back the edges of sandwiches, 'yes. Tomato sandwiches. Now I feel at home.'

Through a window which looked over the porch, Miss Alice Rose materialized at my elbow. She handed me a pitcher of hot water and caught Marjorie's last words. 'My tomato sandwiches are famous throughout the South,' she told us, pronouncing the vegetable with an 'ahh' in the middle. 'The secret to my sandwiches is cutting the toma-to in slices so thin that they are only, just barely, three-dimensional. Then I salt the toma-toes and drain them on cheesecloth. My bread is always fresh and sliced thin, and the butter is unsalted and spread thinly. No matter what people ever said about Alice Rose Cromwell, there's never been anything but admiration for my toma-to sandwiches.' She smiled at us, and disappeared.

In moments, Miss Alice Rose returned, coming through the front door this time, and bearing a silver tea service. 'Last time you were here,' she said, nodding at me, 'the mosquitoes were so bad that sitting out here would have been carnage. They always die off, come September, and I'm ever so pleased to have my porch back. Do you take milk?'

'Just lemon, please.' I watched as Miss Alice Rose placed a half-moon of lemon in my dainty cup, then pressed it against the side of the cup with a silver spoon.

'Even for the South, Miss Alice Rose, you make a ceremony of tea. I don't think I've seen such a lovely table and such elegant food before.' Marjorie sipped at her tea.

'I certainly didn't learn the high art of afternoon nibbling in the South,' responded Miss Alice Rose, leaning back in her chair. She fanned herself with a napkin, then broke a triangular sandwich in half. The filling was cream cheese with pecans and hair-thin strands of carrot, and Miss Alice Rose frowned as the carrot slivers parted indecisively. 'But if I start talking about me, you'll never hear the end of it. Old women ramble, and I am certainly an old woman, and I love to ramble. Tell me about this house you all live in, the one you passed up Singing Pines for.' Miss Alice Rose smiled at me to let me know she understood. 'Are you all happy there?'

So we talked about the beach house, and what we were all doing. Miss Alice Rose listened with interest, interrupting occasionally to ask a question or to chuckle. I watched as Marjorie spoke more, in one afternoon, than I had heard in all the month of August. Slowly nibbling our way through the pastries, we drew the character of our house for Miss Alice Rose. In the middle of laughing over Miles and Katherine's milk fight, Miss Alice Rose hopped up suddenly.

'I forgot the scones,' she said. 'Charred to charcoal briquettes by now, I'd imagine. Excuse me, girls.' She went through the window and her house swallowed her.

I looked helplessly at Marjorie. 'I'm going to explode. I reached over-capacity after my twenty-second sandwich.' In addition to her famed tomato sandwiches, her cream cheese and carrot sandwiches and the odd egg and watercress sandwich, Miss Alice Rose made sandwiches from trout which she smoked herself. Smoked trout, I discovered, was even more delicious than smoked salmon, and I had gorged in a very unladylike fashion.

Marjorie burped. Subdued and soft, it was nonetheless a burp. Given her serene exterior, it seemed inappropriate that such signs of interior warfare should be possible. 'As this is a social occasion', she said, 'I left my watch at home; what time is it?'

I laughed at Marjorie and checked the hour. 'It is now five.'

'Technically, I am meant to be at work at six.'

'We should be going, I think. But I have to say, Marjorie, I am loath to go without hearing Miss Alice Rose speak a bit about herself. Do you realize that we have only talked about the six of us? Perhaps we could corner her in her kitchen. Shall we gather the tea things and give Miss Alice Rose a hand with the dishes?'

But Miss Alice Rose appeared in the mysterious way she had and forbade our assistance. 'Absolutely not,' she said. Then she twinkled. 'Actually, my man will come in and do the dishes. He does the yardwork and helps me around the house. It's a fine thing to have someone to do for you.'

'Is he the reason why you're not lonely, Miss Alice Rose?' I smiled at her uncertainly, hoping that I wasn't being insolent, but feeling very curious.

Marjorie frowned at me infinitesimally. 'You haven't phrased that very well,' she said.

Miss Alice Rose laughed. 'What makes you think I'm not lonely?'

I looked quickly at Marjorie. Sometimes we think along the same lines, and when a similar thought quivers between us, I usually wait for her to select the appropriate words.

'Lonely people only wish to talk about themselves. You are most definitely not a prisoner of your own head, Miss Alice Rose,' Marjorie said. I recognized in the words her appreciation and respect, delicate and rare as wild strawberries.

Miss Alice Rose smiled, making me think again of

French blinds. 'Aren't you both precious,' she said, standing on tip-toe to give our cheeks a kiss. 'I think I'll take that as a compliment. Now, I'm going visiting for the next few weeks, but when I return I want you all to come see me, and bring your friends. Don't stand on ceremony, because when I say come back soon, I mean it, you hear?'

'Thank you very much, Miss Alice Rose!'

She waved us out to the car, and then stood on the porch as we drove away.

Just before we reached the end of the drive, we came upon a huge old Chrysler, parked off on the grass. An elderly man dressed in jeans and a short-sleeved shirt stood, his hands on his hips, staring down at the gloves and steel wool left by Miss Alice Rose. He shook his head back and forth, the negative shakes of resigned irritation. I could see his lips moving, and imagined what he might be saying about Miss Alice Rose.

'Hello,' called Marjorie, lifting her hand in the air and waggling it.

'Howdy,' the man called back, still shaking his head. Then he bent slowly and gathered up the gloves.

'Her man?' I asked Marjorie as we turned out onto the main road.

'Oh, yes,' she said. And we both smiled, first at each other, and then to ourselves.

In mid-September we developed a penchant for sunrises. 'We' is a somewhat misleading pronoun. Not all of us had a great enough desire to rise at six-thirty-eight in the morning. At that hour Miles and Penman could not remove themselves from bed. Sometimes Nathan, looking bleary-eyed and with big hair, came with us. For Marjorie, Katherine, and me, however, very early mornings on the dunes became as much part of our day as feeding the cat or reading the papers.

I have always liked getting up before anything else is moving. The colours which happen when the sky lightens give ordinary objects uncommon interest. When I was very small, I wandered around home right before dawn and noticed things I didn't usually notice, like the very smooth surface of a formica counter. I sat places I didn't usually sit, like atop our piano. Silence is an integral part of early mornings, and so is the readiness of household objects to assume their purposes. Christmas mornings are best in pre-dawn light, because I am sure that any possibility of magic or of unknowable things being revealed comes right before dawn. Supposedly, many people die right before dawn, in what I think is wrongly called the darkest hour. Early mornings have promises to keep.

Mornings at the beach mean me getting up first, usually around five-forty-five. Odious, John Hamden's cat who came with the house, pads out to meet me when I thump down the stairs to the second-floor landing. Odious never goes up to the attic, despite an apparent affection for me and Miles. She alternates nights in Katherine and Nathan's room with an occasional rest on Marjorie's bed. As long as Penman is awake, however, she stays with him. Like Penman, she is at her liveliest in the wee hours of the morning.

Since we arrived at the beach, Penman has undergone revolutionary changes in his feelings towards felines. Penman started out hating cats. At home he has Jack

Russell terriers and those only. Odious has arrogance, though, and a strange sense of fun which appeals to Penman; she also smells much better than his dogs. In fact, given the infrequency of Penman's baths, Odious smells better than Penman. But she is not fastidious, and so the two of them have negotiated an alliance, based at least partially on shared tins of smoked oysters.

Tins of oysters do not a diet make, however. Every morning Odious accompanies me down to the kitchen in happy expectations of further sustenance. Impatiently she waits while I put a kettle on the Aga. Small hard pellets constitute Odious's breakfast, and, after I put them in a bowl for her, she spends the next half hour first ignoring, then applying herself with drooly pleasure to her food. The odour of the bergamot flavouring in my Earl Grey tea almost offsets the smell of cat food.

As my tea steeps I wander around, pausing occasionally to indulge my old habit of sitting in unusual places. There are many different ways to gain perspective, and I suppose sitting on the counter is only one of them. Shortly after six, Katherine comes down. A lovely person for early mornings, she has the grace not to speak until at least six-thirty a.m. Our initial greetings each day are defined by, and limited to, nods and smiles. Early mornings lend Katherine a subtlety she possesses at no other time.

Some time after Odious has finished eating, Marjorie appears. She is an astonishing sight in the dainty pink silk bathrobe her mother insists she wear, a pair of athletic socks, and her bathing suit. Following more nods and two of Marjorie's minimalist smiles, the three of us fill our mugs with tea. Though Katherine would prefer coffee, she possesses a vague notion that tea, minus any sugar or dairy additives, is healthy. But she does not like the taste, and constantly buys new kinds of tea in her search for a palatable potion. So far she has tried and discarded Earl Grey, China, Assam, Darjeeling, Indian, China Black with peach, raspberry and mango flavourings, Lipton iced tea bags, and a variety of Marjorie's herbal tisanes. Quietly, by Katherine's standards, the hunt goes on, with Marjorie occasionally handing Katherine a newly acquired herbal brew to sample.

I believe that the quiet community between the three of us each morning makes our mutual friendship possible. The tension which builds up daily between Katherine and Marjorie disappears as Marjorie hands Katherine an orange and almond tea bag, and Katherine silently smiles her thanks. No questions about whether Marjorie washed her hands or whether the damp night breeze from the ocean has given me sinus problems. As the time approaches sunrise, a contented urgency prevails, though to issue a verbal 'hurry-up' would be unspeakably gauche. Trailing clouds of fragrant steam, we go down to the beach.

The best sunrises come with clouds to reflect the rose and gold glories of sunlight. Perversely, pollution also plays a part in an admirable dawn. The nearby Norfolk shipyards issue chemicals into the air which help make up the colours we see most mornings.

One Sunday morning in mid-September the sun rose without any accompanying clouds. From our vantage point on the dunes we watched, stunned, as it came up fiery red and glowing, like the coil on an electric burner.

'Red sky at morning, sun seekers take warning,' Katherine said irritably, poking a finger as far as she could into her nearly meatless thigh. The poked skin showed a white spot, not appreciably different in hue from the rest of her skin. Katherine has only just begun trying to acquire a tan. The August sun was too close to the earth, in her opinion, for her fear of radiation.

Marjorie looked severe, an expression created by a one-millimeter movement of each eyebrow down towards her nose. 'Old sayings should be abolished, not adapted. Besides, don't the worst burns come on cloudy days, when no one realizes how strong the sun is?'

'Yes, I've always heard that said, and scientifically, I believe it's true.' Katherine looked wistful. 'Somewhere inside of me, though, there is a tanned Barbie-like creature who only believes in sunny days and the smell of coconut oil. I try very hard to smother that persona, but sometimes she rears her head and tosses her long blonde hair.'

I laughed, because that image doesn't fit any part of the Katherine I know, who has short dark hair and who wouldn't come within spitting distance of a saturated fat like coconut oil.

'Of course, Barbie probably died in 1975 of malignant skin tumours which obscured eighty per cent of her body,' continued Katherine. I understood that Sense, not Sensibility, had claimed Katherine back for its own.

Marjorie still frowned at Katherine. 'Don't you wish', she said, as urgently as I've ever seen her, 'that you could wist without needing to be wise?'

'That's a quote, isn't it,' said Katherine.

'Yes. It's a quote from me. I often think that when you speak.' Gradually Marjorie's frown disappeared, along with her vague excitement. Looking at her, Katherine snorted, a whinnying noise, and did not seem to know what to say.

We heard the back screen door bang gently, as though it had only opened a few inches and then fallen back; this was the sign that Odious would shortly accost us. Ever hopeful of having her fur smoothed, Odious often ventures out to the dunes with us, even though she dislikes sand between her paws. Over the rise of the dune, Odious' ears appeared, followed gingerly by the rest of her. After starting in Marjorie's direction for an under-the-ear rub, Odious changed destination mid-course and came to me.

Marjorie examined the day through half-closed eyes. 'It's a lemon pepper pasta day,' she said.

'Excuse me?' said Katherine.

'Lemon pepper pasta comes from a small store two blocks from work. They make their pasta right in front of you. The flavours change daily. I had strawberry *fettucine* yesterday, and they promised me lemon pepper *penne* today.'

'How'd you find the shop?' I wondered. I thought I had mapped out every interesting edible offering for ten miles all around us.

Marjorie smiled her small smile. 'I waited on the shopkeeper's table last week. He and his wife smelled of garlic. When my eyes began to water, they apologized and said they had been making garlic tarragon *tagliatelle* for their store. Nice people. I don't usually wait on people like that.'

Marjorie works in a huge seafood restaurant where families go for all-they-can-eat buffets. Miles and I went once to try the place out. We ate a regrettable platter of 'crispy fried' Alaskan King Crab legs. The whole experience could have been summed up alliteratively as eating cardboard crustaceans in a cavern. Marjorie never partakes of the free meal provided by the restaurant for its employees, and she had advised us not to come for dinner. She said that ordering drinks would be sufficient for us to determine the character of the place. We were more interested in seeing Marjorie at work, though, than we were in savouring our dinner, so it was not a disappointing occasion.

Marjorie chose to work at Happy Jack's the seafood stadium because it was the first place to hire her. She didn't mind the uniform, which was designed to show little skin, or the customers, who were mainly parents dressed in layers of children. Incapable of the bubbly chatter which wrenches tips even from the parsimonious, Marjorie did well by being extraordinarily efficient and by turning over her tables quickly. Miles and I had chuckled to see her summarily squash attempts to flirt with her. She never spoke of personal subjects with customers, and she seldom made character judgements of any sort. I was surprised to hear that she had learned of the pasta shop from her customers, and even more surprised to hear her term the pasta people, 'nice'. From her that was an accolade equalling the purple heart of personality. Thinking about Marjorie's job, I nearly missed her next statement.

'I think when winter comes, and the tourist trade goes completely, I will work at Fettucine by Alfredo,' Marjorie said.

'Is that your pasta shop's name?' asked Katherine.

In reply, Marjorie only blinked. Why speak when you can just stare?

'I think Marjorie feels that you are being offensively obtuse,' I informed Katherine helpfully. Often I feel compelled to intervene between the two of them. Communication between Marjorie and Katherine is a curious thing; Katherine's words to Marjorie are fired off like bowling balls which veer off to the gutter before ever approaching the tenpins of Marjorie's brain. Marjorie's words resemble lunar moths which flutter right over Katherine's head. Occasionally I feel like an interpreter.

'I wonder how much difference winter will make to our incomes?' Katherine wasn't really asking for an answer, or even for concerted speculation. She just needs to inject some angst into even the most peaceful of situations. None of us were particularly worried about the lack of winter customers. Life in Virginia Beach goes on even when the summer people leave. Except for Marjorie, we all worked in places whose cashflows had steady diets of local customers, rather than relying solely on tourists. Now that Marjorie had prospects of a winter job, it seemed we were all settled.

The morning winds were dying as the sun gained in the sky. Heat rose around us in visible waves and the hot bugs began to trill. Heeding the call of cool flagstones, Odious went back to the porch, there to lie sprawled and groggy with four paws in the air.

'I need to swim.' Marjorie shrugged out of her bathrobe and stood up. The heat made her hair curl wildly, and she was having trouble collecting it to lift off her neck.

'Wait a second, please,' Katherine said. Marjorie wilted gracefully back on the sand. I'm sure her mother regrets that swooning has gone out of style.

'Nathan's got a problem, and he won't talk about it; he wouldn't at all like me saying anything to you about him, but I can't help it. I'm concerned, and I think you should be, too.' As if she'd known what she wanted to say for a long time, Katherine spoke in a torrent. Silent, we listened and took advantage of having a serious conversation in the sand. Serious conversations are best held where hands have something to do. Though fields of grass are good places, sand dunes are even better. Katherine's hands automatically made sand hillocks and swept them away.

Even before Katherine spoke, I knew what we were going to talk about. Nathan has diabetes. Would it be unfair to say that Katherine could only love someone who gave her something legitimate to fret about? I can't say for certain that Katherine actively enjoys worrying, but it is her habit, her mental tic. Nathan's disease provides fodder to feed her worries, especially since Nathan possesses such a cavalier attitude toward his illness.

During our senior year of college, Nathan seldom found the time to take care of himself properly. He wrapped himself in his honours thesis, a 190-page treatise on the movement toward democratic leadership among rebel groups in South American countries. After visiting Nicaragua and Guatemala on our Thanksgiving break, he came back with a tropical intestinal disease other than the usual one. For the next few months his exotic stomach disorders pursued him with virulent intent.

In mid-December of last year, Katherine accused him of actively trying to kill himself. Nathan was getting himself locked into the library each night so that he could have unrestricted use of the college's limited number of personal computers. Afraid that Nathan might forget to eat and sleep, Katherine used to pack him a backpack for his overnight library sojourns. The backpack had a pillow, an alarm clock, a thermos of hot chocolate, and chicken sandwiches which were Katherine's speciality – a mix of Indian spices, grapes, and yoghurt on brown bread. Nathan was never ungrateful, but as often as not, the provisions were barely touched.

Last year at Christmas, Nathan went to the hospital in a diabetic coma. His mother called Katherine, who immediately drove from Atlanta to Nathan's home in Savannah. From Savannah she called Penman, whom she could trust to spread the word among us. 'He is still unconscious,' Penman relayed. He reported Katherine's words verbatim. 'She said she told him Merry Christmas anyway, and that if he ever behaves this foolishly again, she will do him in before his blood sugar ever gets the chance.' Penman had spoken cautiously, and had added that Katherine sounded unusually emotional. Exasperated, I told him I couldn't imagine why.

Nathan survived Christmas, his 'Fool Yule', as Katherine dubbed it. Once again conscious, he received firm instructions on modifying his lifestyle. His doctors assured him of dire consequences if he ignored the warning inherent in his collapse. Though Nathan listened, and tried to follow the advice, he has never been able to accept his illness completely; perhaps mortality is a hard concept for a person like Nathan to accept. The schedule he likes to keep would reduce even a completely healthy person to rubble. Nathan says he can't find a way to get everything done in any less time.

I'm not sure that Nathan thinks he's impervious to mortality, as Katherine theorizes. Marjorie and I think that life isn't worth much to Nathan if he can't live without restrictions. My wise old Grandad says that life is a compromise. He says that while mixing up a wicked potion of peach brandy, fresh orange juice, and lemon vodka that is his version of a fuzzy navel. We toast each other and the fuzzy navels flow freely through Grandad's hardened arteries. I don't know what compromises Grandad makes. I know Nathan doesn't make many.

How Nathan spent the interval between graduation and coming to Virginia Beach is only for Nathan to know. At our initial 'what have you been doing' confabulation, Nathan only said that he had been 'fighting for truth, justice and the American way', and rolled his eyes. He looked tired when he first came to the beach, and he looked even more tired now.

Katherine was finally ready to speak. She cleared her throat and patted the sand softly, her fingers flat and held close together, like a spatula. She looked at Marjorie and me.

Marjorie looked back at her. '"Language is the music with which we charm the serpents guarding another's treasure." That's Ambrose Bierce telling you to spit it out. Do you know Ambrose Bierce? He was both a Southern writer – unjustly neglected by history – and a professional cynic. My grandmother would think my choice of authors and of words very unladylike.' She sipped her tea.

'All right. Nathan's shift ended last night at midnight. He did not get home until two because he stayed to clean ovens and to get overtime pay. He had dinner with me then, and gave himself an injection only after I reminded him. I think', said Katherine slowly, 'that he's being careless on purpose. Last night when we fell asleep on the couch, I wasn't sure that he hadn't lost consciousness.'

'To the best of my knowledge, that's an integral part of sleeping,' said Marjorie solemnly.

Flicking her a glance of supreme irritation, Katherine said, 'It's not amusing, Marjorie. Though I don't know why I bother telling you that. You don't live life, you *float* through it.'

Marjorie merely shrugged her shoulders. In order for one person to insult another, both individuals must share a similar frame of reference. I almost smiled thinking that to Marjorie, floating through life probably equalled a compliment. Conscious of the duties of friendship, however, I composed myself and made the necessary reply. 'Nathan knows the risks, Katherine.' I found a shell in the hole I was digging and buried it in the small mound I'd dug out.

'I don't care about him knowing the risks. I care about him not *caring* about the risks.' Katherine wrecked my hillock with her foot.

'"This is something up with which I will not put"' quoted Marjorie. 'Winston Churchill. He wasn't Southern, but he was still a gentleman.'

Katherine looked at her crossly. 'Do you really think that's applicable?' she asked.

'"Remain as I do, incomprehensible,"' said Marjorie, 'Oscar Wilde.'

Katherine looked about to say something else, but then the door banged on the back porch. It was a big noise, not like the gentle closing of a door just opened wide enough for a cat. Only one other person would be up before nine o'clock on a weekend morning. The object of our discussion appeared, hirsute and happy, over the dunes.

'This is a great morning for a swim,' Nathan said. 'And whoever found the innovative tea with the little dried flowers in it has made my day. You couldn't pay me to drink the stuff, but I enjoyed watching the flowers bloom in the water. My cup is still sitting there, so you can all admire them as well. For a proper brew, I'll have to wait 'til Miles stirs.'

Katherine had found a box of chrysanthemum tea at an oriental grocery store. Though the tea looked very pretty, brewing and sipping it was roughly comparable to boiling and drinking potpourri. Not a tantalizing gourmet experience.

Nathan must have heard us out on the dunes. Squatting and squawking like a trio of hag seagulls, we'd been out here for nearly an hour. But he didn't ask us for the content of our conversation. Perhaps that was just the kind of courtesy Nathan practises. Perhaps he knew we had been speaking about him. For Katherine, however, the conversation had been like coughing up a fishbone, and we had only gotten halfway through. She still had a bone to choke on. Like the heat, her tension quivered in the air.

'For someone going to sleep at three a.m., this is extremely early to be up. Human bodies don't function without rest,' Katherine said.

Nathan smiled at her. 'You are one to talk, ma. Who had dinner with me at two a.m.? Give me a break. It's too hot to sleep. I don't know how Miles and Penman manage it. Come swim.' Nathan slipped a rubber band off his wrist and gathered his hair into it. He always says that if he leaves his hair unbound in the water, it gets in his eyes and feels like seaweed on his shoulders. My own tresses are quite long, and I sympathize with the feeling. Standing on the dunes and plaiting my hair, I watched while Marjorie, Katherine, and Nathan headed down to the water.

Katherine's back looked stiff as she followed the other two. Once made angry, for whatever reason, Katherine takes ages to cool to room temperature. While Nathan and Marjorie splashed into the water, she hung back. Poor Katherine. For her most things are serious, because she sees the seeds of destruction everywhere. Very early this morning, Nathan had scared her enough to provoke anger. What was she afraid of? Wondering, I fastened the end of my braid with a rubber band and trundled down to the water's edge.

We caught the tide as it was heading out, a very warm and quiet tide. Out beyond the second sandbar, porpoises rose in arcs and flashes. We watched them before going into the water ourselves.

'I wonder what they gave up?' Marjorie asked aloud, her attention focused like a beam on the porpoises.

'In order to be like that? Some of the more fanciful biologists say it was the opposable thumb. Did you ever read *The Once and Future King*? I think it was by T. H. White.' I was asking Marjorie, really, but to my surprise Katherine nodded her head immediately.

'I didn't like T. H. White, but we read him in freshman literature. You're talking about that little rodent's story, where he tells how all the animals chose their body parts to suit a certain purpose, like the mole and his nose for digging. Man didn't ask for any gift.'

'So he suits all purposes?' said Nathan, smiling at Katherine.

'Something like that,' I said.

'I'd like to touch one.' Marjorie had not taken her eyes from the water, where the porpoises appeared intermittently.

We had stood long enough in the surf that the salt spray was drying on my body. It made me itch. Taking great strides I moved forward until the water was high enough to resist me, then with relief I fell in. The swim out to the first sandbar was a short one, and when I stood up, Nathan threw a Frisbee out to me. We played a noisy game of keep away which brought

Miles out of the house. He was simultaneously trying to eat a bagel and to run; the combination, helped by post-pillow coordination, likened him to a defective battery-operated dog. He gave in to his bagel and sat on the shore to finish it. After splashing in to see him, I received a cream cheese kiss for my trouble. We watched the other three leap for the Frisbee and tumble in the small surf.

'Katherine's worried about him,' I told Miles quietly and nodded my head in Nathan's direction.

Miles fished with his tongue for a blob of cream cheese resting on his upper lip. The blob was stubborn; razor stubble gave it traction. Miles wanted to know if it was Nathan whom we had been discussing so intently in the dunes this morning.

'How did you know?' I asked him; he sounded as though he had seen us.

'I woke up early and had to go to the bathroom. Saw you out the window,' Miles said.

'You've just epitomized the mysteries of maleness, Miles. No female would understand your lack of a need to *know*. Had you been a woman peering out of the window, the sight of us on the sand would have limbered up your curiosity. Had you been subtle, you would have quickly made toast and brought it out to us, thereby bribing your way into our privacy.' I shook my head at him.

'Yes,' said Miles, chewing and gulping, 'but had I been tired, which I was, I would have gone straight back to bed, which I did. Besides, why learn things which you might not want to know. Girl talk always leads to someone finding out more than they want to.'

'What do you mean? Have you wondered about Nathan yourself?' This was interesting. If Miles worried about Nathan, that was different from just Katherine feeling anxious.

'I've wondered about Nathan since last Christmas,' said Miles reluctantly. 'He hasn't been too concerned about taking care of himself since then. Maybe he learned something at the hospital after he came out of the coma.'

'I can't believe you haven't said anything before now.' Miles' observation disturbed me, all the more because it emerged despite his natural reticence. And suddenly, I was furious. 'Communication is an ordinary function of humanity, Miles. Why are you such an asshole?'

'Don't be angry. I just didn't want anyone bothering Nathan about something that is pure speculation on my part. It's Nathan's own business what he tells us.'

'So he hasn't *said* anything about it to you . . . ?' I asked.

'No. Here, have a bite. The jam is some wild blueberry stuff which mom sent from her medical convention in Bangor. We have a care package full of Vermont maple syrup and preserves and salsa from the Maine Maid in Damariscotta. I've put most of it in the pantry to use later, but the blueberry jam is in the refrigerator for everyone to sample. I hope no one else likes it.'

Miles isn't selfish, but he's an almost professional hoarder. He also knows that food is the best way to distract me from something he doesn't want to talk about. Of all the rational people I have met,

Miles is the most infuriatingly reasonable. Fighting with him provides no satisfaction whatsoever; what artichokes are to the vegetable kingdom, Miles is to the argumentative field — lots of work, little reward, and I'm never certain how to deconstruct either one.

'Catch!' Winging a Frisbee toward Miles and me, Nathan shouted to attract our attention. Miles leapt for the disc at the same time as I did, and we both fell sprawling and spluttering into the surf. There followed a vigorous game of keep away.

None of us had to be at work before noon. Noon on Sunday is a difficult time to have to pursue gainful employment. Sundays are for reading newspapers and for trying new recipes, for yodelling along with Aaron Copeland's music, played loudly to the distress of the cat.

Except for Miles, we all work in the 'hospitality' industry. As a Southerner, Penman finds the term 'hospitality industry' both euphemistic and oxymoronic — with the emphasis on moronic. It's euphemistic, he says, to label fast food as hospitality, and it's oxymoronic to put 'hospitable' next to industry. Penman thinks hospitality isn't to be paid for, and it can't be produced like hairpins or hamburgers and labelled as industry.

I agree with Penman in that the hospitality industry isn't hospitable to the people who work in it, since in many cases, the labour of hospitality goes on twenty-four hours a day, 365 days each year. Waffle Houses are eternal, and truckstops are timeless. Bars and restaurants like the ones where we ply our trades are merely interminable. Weekends certainly aren't sacred, but that works to our financial advantage. On a busy Saturday night, Katherine, who has graduated to tending the bar at the Kudzu Cafe, can make more money than she makes all the rest of the week put together.

Sunday afternoons and Sunday nights, though, are very slow. The customer base comprises the reluctant to go back to work, the reluctant to indulge, to overindulge, and the reluctant to spend any money. On Sundays women have drinks with men to whom they would never have devoted a Friday or a Saturday night. On Sundays, families come out to sip iced tea.

For waiters and waitresses, who have their own sub-culture and jargon, Sundays are a time to discuss the weekend's tips and to complain about the schedule for the week ahead. Some of the staff have children who they miss seeing on Sundays. They miss seeing their kids on Friday and Saturday too, but Friday and Saturday nights pay for food and rent. Sunday pays for cat food and candy bars. Sundays are gloomy times for the hospitality industry.

I wasn't due for work until one p.m. The only thing more reprehensible than working on a Sunday is working on a Sunday while wearing a uniform composed of an electric blue lycra mini-skirt and an electric blue blouse covered with electric every other colour squiggles. The manager of the restaurant, The Raven's Roost, chose our uniforms because she thought them 'cheerful', 'I love these colours,' she had said with her eyes bugging out hugely. 'It's sort of "I sing the Body Eclectic".'

My manager bears and suits the name Helen Wildly. Most restaurant owners in Virginia Beach have employed her at some time to whip their establishments into profitability. Helen smiles like a shark and is everywhere, all the time. Her staff like her because she's fair. Customers like her because she makes them feel lucky to be in her restaurant. I had liked her immediately on meeting her, and she had sized me up, then offered to employ our whole house. Only Penman took her up on her offer. Everyone else had already found a job. She and Penman get on very well. Having discerned that Penman has no need whatsoever for the considerable money he makes as a bartender, she likes him even better for doing his job superbly.

The Raven's Roost is Helen Wildly's most successful operation yet, combining decent food and drink with a waterside site. A huge back porch connected to the bar extends out over a lagoon, and the nearby marina provides entertainment in the form of boats which draw up with sharks dangling bloodily from deep sea poles. At rest on the porch, and drinking copious draughts, beefy businessmen survey their catches with glee. On Friday and Saturday nights the whole place fills until it stands still, and the bartenders go mad making sweet shooters with suggestive names.

Penman works behind the bar where racks of glasses and a four-foot wall of wood insulate him from customers. He is free, there, to watch everyone and to murmur lines to himself from *The Beautiful and Damned* or *The Great Gatsby*. He thinks F. Scott Fitzgerald would have liked The Raven's Roost. Once, to humour Penman, I asked him why.

'It's a matter of "dispensing starlight to casual moths",' he said.

Detachment is not possible for cocktail waitresses, however. I am out among the tables taking orders and sashaying along with a tray of dirty glasses and tall frozen drinks. I've learned how to balance my tray properly – one-handed with fingers curved and fanned along the underside of the tray, half of which rests on the heel of my hand. A waitress named Debbie taught me to carry a glass of water at all times. That way, when the back deck gets very crowded and I can't get anyone to move out of my way, I can tip a trickle of water on the person directly in front of me. The person moves quickly, propelled by a fear that a whole tray of drinks may shortly follow where the cold wet drops went. I bat my eyes and bulldoze through, and no one yet has wised to our crowd control technique.

Despite all the hilarity, The Raven's Roost is often a grim place. Lots of people come because they have no place else to go. If you had no money and were in that kind of quandary, you might end up under a newspaper on some street corner. If you have money, though, you might end up at a bar. I watch people buy drinks for people who don't ever reciprocate. People of all sexes slink off with other people of all sexes. Social diseases have a presence here. When I'm feeling exceedingly depressed, however, the kitchen makes a tasty baked brie which brightens my world view. Penman says I see the world through carbohydrate-coloured glasses. Perhaps I'm not the only one. After closing, Helen Wildly often sits with Penman and me to eat brie and talk. Helen gets tippled on a very fine cognac reserved mostly for her. Sometimes Miles comes to join us, and we all concoct new drinks. Roaming the length of some 200 bottles we put pear brandy into the makings of a classic margarita or try a combination of chambord, sambucca, and cream. Helen puts the costs of our efforts down to research and considers it a bargain. One of our concatenations, the 'Mariner's Stiffy', became the bar's most popular drink despite a hefty five-dollar price tag.

Sometimes our chats and experimentation continue on until the late wee hours. Helen has, by that time, folded on to her arms on top of the bar, and one of us takes her home. On Sunday nights Helen tries not to come in. Sunday nights are usually very quiet, and Helen should feel comfortable leaving the place in the slightly moist but probably capable hands of The Raven's Roost's owner, Norton Marley. But most Sunday nights find Helen seated at a table on the deck. Though she pretends to be a customer, she is still the manager. Alcoholic, workaholic, she scares us even while her sense of purpose attracts us. Helen Wildly is the one person I know who would rather be working on Sunday night.

From the dunes by the back patio, Katherine called to us that the hour for elevenses had arrived. For everyone else that meant iced tea and oatmeal cookies. I think elevenses is one of Katherine's less obvious efforts to keep Nathan eating small amounts all day, thereby regulating his blood sugar. This morning's elevenses meant to me that the time had come for a shower and a thorough deodorizing before a long hot shift in my electric blues. On my way upstairs, I called to Nathan that if he wanted a ride to work, he would have to be ready at eleven-forty five. I didn't think he heard me, but I knew Katherine would tell him. The wind tunnel which doubles as our staircase to the attic puffed a mat of sticky salt hair into my eyes, and I nearly fell up the last two steps.

Virginia Beach's water always smells vaguely of eggs when the first steam rises off a trickle from the hot tap. I have never figured out whether the smell quickly dissipates, or, whether the sulphuric odour of farts is one to which humans readily acclimatize. Eggs or not, few things make me feel as clean as a shower after playing in sea water, especially since the salinity level in our sheltered bay rivals that of pickle juice. Clean is something best appreciated by the dirty. No wonder people sing in the shower.

Miles came in to the bathroom just as I started to hum. His hand, holding a cookie, snaked around the edge of the shower curtain. Snatching the cookie, I avoided wet oatmeal by stuffing it whole into my mouth.

'Now that your mouth is full, and you won't be able to answer me right away, I need to say something you are not going to like. Please leave Nathan alone. Don't bother him about something being wrong. He'll tell us when and if he needs to. You're thinking about talking to him, and I just think it would be better if you didn't.' Miles was seated on the toilet, speaking softly to the spot behind the curtain where he reckoned I was standing. I was listening, and I was annoyed, more at his manipulation than anything else. Frustrated, I stood in the shower, my mouth crammed with cookie and my sight obscured by shampoo suds. All over me the water washed the salt away.

'Oooph,' I managed.

'Hmmm,' said Miles. 'Yes, sticks and stones will break my bones, but names don't hurt unless you can pronounce them.'

I chewed and swallowed with monumental effort. 'I wasn't calling you anything nasty, but who do you think I am? Give me some credit for tact. And, besides, don't you think you're making too large an issue out of this? Why shouldn't Nathan talk about what's bothering him, if something really is?'

'It's his business,' Miles said, shaking his head.

'When we all live together like we are, one person's business is every person's business, especially if that business affects us all.' I was spitting cookie crumbs and they were soggy around my toes.

'Business is what my mother called the stuff that the dog did in the back yard when I was little. "Don't bother Moggie, he's doing business," Mom would tell me,' said Miles.

'Two questions I have for you. Why'd you call your dog by a cat's name, and what does your little reminiscence make you as a "business man"? I was smiling as I reached for a towel and whipped the shower curtain back.

'Hmmm,' said Miles again.

I strapped my watch on after a glance told me it was eleven-thirty-five. Upstairs in the attic, the electric blues flew on with unusual speed. As I hurried back down to the landing I patted my wet footprints off the floor with my towel. Miles was still in the bathroom but the door was closed.

'What are you doing?' I called.

'"Business",' was Miles' bemused reply.

'Oh, dear, I've got to go, Miles. I'll see you later.'

'I'm ready,' called Nathan from the kitchen.

'Happy Sunday!' I told Miles through the closed door.

The weatherman had predicted a hot and breezy afternoon, so the daytrippers clogged the roads with a vengeance. Though Labour Day Weekend was two weekends ago, and was to have signified the official end of summer, unofficially summer wouldn't end till the air was cold enough so that people wouldn't come from as far away as Washington to enjoy an afternoon at the beach. Labour Day did signify the end of the season for white shoes, though. I informed Nathan of this fact. He wore white tennis shoes.

'You're living a lie,' he said comfortably.

'What?'

'The only purpose of etiquette is to make a structure for the way privileged people live. It gives them something to do. Etiquette differs from manners in that the sole purpose of manners is to make people comfortable. It's etiquette to know where a fingerbowl should be placed on a table; it's manners to drink from yours if you notice that your guest thinks his is a water dish. Wearing white shoes only between Memorial Day and Labour Day is etiquette. Etiquette and affectation are synonymous.' Having delivered himself of his soliloquy, Nathan crossed his legs and flicked a speck of something gooey off his white shoes. Since the flick was ineffective, he set to work scraping with his fingernail.

Nathan's Pizza Hut occupies a short stretch of

highly commercial territory about five minutes from the house. Sometimes Nathan bicycles to work, but more often one of us takes him. He did not own a car to bring to the beach. When we arrived at the Pizza Hut, a group of teenage girls carrying signs met us in the parking lot. The girls were all wearing very minute bikinis and their signs said: 'Discriminatory'; 'Unfair'; and 'Down with Pizza Hut.'

'Have you been having a labour dispute?' I asked Nathan.

'No. Those are former customers who are taking exception to the fact that they were not allowed to dine whilst wearing bathing suits and sandals. They said that the sign on the door only requires shirts and shoes.'

'Some of those girls barely have on a top, certainly not a top that qualifies as a shirt,' I said.

'Ah,' said Nathan, looking appreciative. 'No one objects to the cleavage.' I raised my eyebrows, but he continued.

'The issue is that those bikini bottoms, "shorts" the young civil disobedients call them, have the thickness and effectiveness of g-strings. As swimming trunks they have all the substantial air of dental floss applied to the lower regions. The waitresses were complaining about having to wipe pubic hairs off the seats.'

'I think I'm going to be ill. Nathan, I get off work around nine. Do you want me to stop by to see if you need a ride home?'

'No,' he said. 'I may be home before that tonight. I'll walk back. Thanks for the ride. Wish me luck braving the picketers.'

I watched him wade through the controversially-clad teenagers who enjoined him to join in their strike. Nathan good-naturedly shook his braid at them and passed on inside.

'Sublimate your energies,' he told them. 'Call for tighter controls on North Sea whaling or lobby against abortion restrictions. You can rise above this.'

They shook their chests at him and thrust their placards higher.

Penman came to join me at work just after five o'clock. By the time he arrived, an unusually large Sunday crowd had thinned considerably, leaving me with the leisure to notice Penman's nose. His olfactory organ sported a lurid pink tint which went well with the squiggles on his electric blue shirt. I spoke to him each time I had to go to the service bar for drinks.

'Were you actually up in time to get some sun?' I asked him as a powerful blender mixed a fresh strawberry daiquiri.

Penman patted his nose tenderly. 'For a number of hours, Marjorie and I engaged in a bitter contest of backgammon out on the beach. Katherine and Miles found a baby octopus in a pile of flotsam. It seemed tangled and tired, so they brought it up to the kitchen tank to recuperate.'

The kitchen tank was becoming a major source of amusement. John Hamden left it for us, dismantled in a cupboard. He told us that if we could resuscitate it, we could use it as a saltwater base camp for marine specimens. Apparently, the whole set-up belonged to a former girlfriend who kept carnivorous turtles in it.

John Hamden said the girl and the turtles were eating him out of house and home, so he got rid of them. The girl went to Nebraska, and the turtles went to the sea. After setting up the tank we'd started a saltwater collection; an octopus was a new tenant for us.

'Have they named it yet?' I slit a strawberry and set it on the rim of the daiquiri. Penman began on a frozen vodka lemonade.

'I think it will be christened Ignatius. Katherine wished to call the creature Pampas, after the grass clump in which it was ensnared. Miles said that would be traumatic, like calling a little Soviet orphan with three arms "Chernobyl". I suggested Ignatius. I've been reading up on martyrs.'

Penman put the second drink on my tray, and, after plopping a lemon curl atop it, I set both drinks down in front of my two favourite customers, an aging director and his elegant female assistant. The director tipped me twice as much as the drinks cost. Gleefully I wandered off to the kitchen to inquire about rumoured price increases in the restaurant's selection of hors d'oeuvres.

On any evening other than Sunday, Penman would not have time to talk to me while he filled my frozen drinks order. While the blender whirred he would have been washing glasses, opening beers, ringing up orders for bar customers, and frantically shifting cases of coffee cream into the coolers. The Raven's Roost's clientele drinks plenty of cream drinks — Kahlua and creams, amaretto and creams, Brandy Alexanders, and shooters with cream floating on top. It is a sticky, sweet and oily crowd on the whole.

On any night other than a Sunday, I would not have time to talk to Penman, or to investigate rumours in the kitchen. My usual allotment of tables is six. Six tables can mean up to fifty people, depending on the level of the crowd. The only way to keep them all served is to never waste a moment. I clear my tables while drink orders are being filled, and run to the kitchen to pick up cheese plates and clams casino.

Some of the waitresses pay less attention to customers who don't look like good tippers. They must have more faith than I in the ability to spot generous people. One of my first nights I expected no tip from a young couple with a baby who ordered cheaply. They left me a thirty per cent tip. Two middle-aged women, notoriously dreadful tippers, left me four dollars on a ten dollar bill. I decided shortly thereafter that, commercially, I was a rotten judge of character. So now I treat everyone the same and end up solvent.

After a thoroughly unexciting evening, enlivened only by a new waitress who upended a tray of Bloody Marys all over a woman's white linen suit, I headed for home. It was about ten p.m. As I left, Penman was discussing Andy Warhol with a fuddled gentleman who claimed he'd given old Andy the inspiration for his Campbell's soup cans. Penman earns his tips. Waving, I strolled away.

Out in the parking lot, I stopped to stare at a huge moon which was rising slowly over the street lamps. Beach moons are generally smooth and white, as if the salt air has bleached them and water has washed the rough edges away. I guess most moons appear smooth and white. But it's only at the beach that a logical explanation exists for the smooth white facade.

I drove home and found Miles, in his pyjamas, preparing a taco salad and drinking Mexican brew – a Sol.

'Do you know, at The Raven's Roost we were using some fifty cases of Sol on busy nights until a rumour circulated that Mexican beer contains twenty per cent human urine. Now we still sell 1200 bottles of Sol a night, but everyone uses chunks of lime to sterilize it. I thought you hated Mexican beer. Where's Nathan?'

'Not very good at sticking on one subject are you? Nathan's not home yet. And yes, I do dislike Mexican beer,' said Miles. 'But it seemed wrong, somehow, to drink a Rolling Rock with Mexican food. Did you have a good evening?'

'It was long, but not bad for a Sunday night.' I examined the fish tank, searching for Ignatius the Octopus.

'If you're looking for our new addition, check behind the filter. He hides out there. Squished.'

'Oh! Miles, he looks very sad. Jules Verne must have had quite an imagination to see this as a beast who could wreck a submarine. Do you think Ignatius is reconciled to his name? He looks more like a Jim or a Floyd to me.'

'Whoever he is, I think he needs to go back to the sea tomorrow. I'm not sure we can feed him adequately here. Penman will have a spell. He seems to have adopted it as some kind of a familiar.'

'More likely he wants to keep it for squid's ink pasta, or something equally exotic. Do octopi produce ink like squid do?'

Miles didn't know, so we watched in silence for a while. The bubbles from the aquarium's filter made a restful noise, and Miles rubbed the back of my neck expertly. Eventually, he went back to his taco salad, where he was at the guacamole stage. He minced up onion and garlic, then sprinkled them with fresh lemon juice. After finely chopping some cherry tomatoes, he peeled an avocado. Dumping all the ingredients into a bowl, Miles then began to squeeze them together through his fingers. He pulled the avocado pit away from the mash and continued oozing together the mixture. A pale green mess formed which slid through his fingers with the alacrity of mud.

'I suppose people normally do this with a spoon,' said Miles, who saw my fascinated disgust. 'You don't get the same texture, though, not even with a food processor.' He scraped each finger on the edge of the bowl and went to wash his hands. For someone whose repertoire extends only to sandwiches and taco salads, Miles has an unusual number of culinary obsessions.

The guacamole was transferred to a bed of lettuce atop a scattering of blue corn tortilla chips. Carefully, Miles arranged layers of tomatoes, refried beans, salsa, and sour cream. On the very top he set a mound of chicken breast which had been marinated in chilli oil and tequila, then pan-fried and shredded. He smiled at me as he got two forks and picked up his opus. I noticed he took care first to set aside the bowl used for mixing his avocado glop.

'Penman insists on licking anything that sticks to the sides,' Miles said.

We went out to the back porch, where the mess

we made wouldn't matter nearly so much. As soon as we finished we went up to bed. Miles had to be in Washington by eight-thirty on Monday morning to examine a company which manages a small chain of dismal pet shops. In order to arrive on time, he would have to leave the house before dawn, by five-fifteen at the latest.

Miles did his usual ten-minute grumble about how the human body only functions efficiently upon having had eight hours of sleep. It's one of the few things about which he agrees with Katherine. This pre-pillow patter is Miles' equivalent of counting sheep, and I am so accustomed to it that I don't have to listen. Subconsciously I know when to make small affirmative 'mmm' noises even while my attention is fixed elsewhere. With small winds puffing out the curtains and the sucking noise of a quiet tide filling our heads, we fell asleep.

4

Refried beans and bed rest closely juxtaposed play havoc with the digestive juices. By two a.m. mine were frothing and foaming at the mouth of my large intestine, so to speak. I got out of bed quietly and headed for the comfort of a cracker and some Coke. There are very few occasions when the advice my grandmother gave me when I was five actually has a place in my existence. This however, was one of them. The pains in my stomach called for that antiquated cure to settle them.

Downstairs all was quiet and dark. Marjorie and Katherine and Nathan were probably in bed asleep. Penman wouldn't be home for another hour. Some moonlight illuminated the kitchen, but not enough to guide me in a search through the pantry. I snapped on an overhead light.

An 'umphh' came from the couch in the corner of the kitchen. 'That's bright,' came the source of the 'umphh'.

Blinking my eyes at the light, I concentrated on using sheer will power to adjust my pupils. I don't know whether that helps much with pupil adjustment, but in seconds I could see that the sounds came from Nathan, sitting upright and wide-awake on the middle of the sofa. He still wore his red and grey pizza uniform. On his face was the peaceful look of someone who has been in the same place for a long time. Odious, who loves sedentary lapses in her housemates, was settled with her hindquarters on Nathan's lap and her head on a cushion at Nathan's side. She lay belly up and had one paw raised in a sort of feline salute. Nathan was scratching her armpit. She looked blissful.

'There's a pepperoni and black olive pizza in the refrigerator if you're feeling hungry,' Nathan said.

'I think my insides would mutiny. That would have been very tasty before Miles' taco salad, though. I thought you would be home early tonight. When did you get back?'

'About one a.m.,' he said.

'Did Katherine wait up to nag at you for staying at work too late and neglecting your health?'

'No,' he said and smiled with patience. 'She left a very thorough note instead.'

I wanted my cracker very badly now. I had found Coke and ice and a glass, and now I just wanted a very plain cracker. A package of water biscuits lay open in the pantry and I began to chew. Nathan watched me, smiling.

'My grandma says there is nothing better than a cracker and a cola to settle an upset stomach,' he told me.

'My grandmother said the same thing. I guess you have to know certain things before you graduate to grandmotherhood. I'm excited about being a grandmother, but I'd like to do it without being a mother first. Can you imagine me in maternity gear?'

'I think you'll have a problem with that. Does Miles know you're not thrilled about having kids?'

'Oh, please, Nathan, just to talk about marriage gives Miles hives. The subject of kids would leave him speechless. Maybe that's because it supposedly costs a quarter of a million dollars to raise a child to the age of twenty-one. Do you and Katherine talk about children?'

All around the edge of my cracker I nibbled, taking bites so small I could taste individual granules of salt. The Coke tasted like Coke only does when I need one rather than just casually reach for one.

'You assume that Katherine and I talk about marriage. Everyone always thinks that the way things are now lasts forever. We're not having children. I can't,' said Nathan.

'The question which this conversation begs for is "why". "Why, Nathan can't you have children?" But I won't ask that. 'Cause I have another question. What's wrong with you, Nathan? You never sleep, you look ill, you stay up late in the dark feeling contemplative in your Pizza Hut uniform. Miles made me promise I wouldn't bug you on this, so I'll only ask once.'

'When I was very young,' Nathan said, 'my grandad died after having had a *terminal illness*. You know how you are when you first start hearing words and you know that they are new and important. *Terminal illness* were two words like that. I liked to use them. I knew it meant he was dying, but the meaning, as it applied to me, was pretty distant. I hadn't seen Grandad for years and he was dying on the other side of the country. When he died, I cried not for him but for me, because it was all very mysterious and I didn't understand. There was also a little drama involved. Those words, *terminal illness*, made me feel important.

'Even after Grandad died I still thought *terminal illness* was a kind of disease, and I wondered why there wasn't a *terminal illness* telethon, like Jerry Lewis did for muscular dystrophy.' Nathan smiled, sort of inwardly and at himself. Absentmindedly he rubbed Odious' ear, and, as he had been doing the same ear for three minutes solid, she punished him by sinking her teeth into his wrist.

'Damn cat,' said Nathan. With the dignity of the offended, Odious leapt from his lap. She stalked to the base of the refrigerator where warm air puffed out of the grill, and there she settled into a crouch. Her face and ears had the perverse set cats assume to indicate that anyone who touches them is meatloaf. I respected her wishes.

'I'm dying,' said Nathan.

And strangely, the tranquillity of the kitchen remained undisturbed. Nathan, too, looked undisturbed. 'I am telling you now because you are here and I feel like saying it. At twenty-four years old I am dying of pancreatic cancer and there really isn't anything to do about it. For a long time I thought I "only" had diabetes.' He stopped speaking for a moment. 'It is', he said, 'a real crock of shit.'

'Jesus Christ,' I said, and Odious sprawled in the warm, Freon-flavoured flatus of the refrigerator, and the kettle sat on the back of the stove as it always does, and the wood floor continued to lie golden knotty smooth and smelling of Murphy's oil soap. Tra la la la life goes on.

Irrationally, I was angry. 'Nathan, you asshole, I should have expected this before now. I should have *known* five minutes ago when you told me about your grandfather. How can you just drop this . . . ugh.' A stab of pain implied the inadequacy of crackers and Coke. Nathan unfolded himself from the couch and went to get another Coke out of the refrigerator for me. Odious didn't like having to move, but Nathan was definite about opening the refrigerator door. He examined the insides.

'I've known about this for nine months now, so I've had all the reactions you expect, and now I just accept it. I will die, I will not *pass over*, and it will simply happen to me long before it happens to the rest of you. If any of you ever refer to me after I'm dead as "passed over", or even worse, "passed away", I'll find a way to return for a horrible haunting.

'The only way for me to deal with this is honestly, and to keep it all in proportion. I know what I'm going to miss, and how much. I've practised saying unpleasant words over and over, and now they seem normal. Not Katherine's definition of normal, but a special one I've developed for the occasion.' Nathan directed his speech to an orange juice container inside the refrigerator. After moving a pizza box aside, he found a single cold can of Coke encircled by a ring of half-full cat food cans. We are always opening new cans of cat food because we forget to check for old ones. Besides, Penman won't feed Odious cold food. He invariably prepares a fresh can.

Nathan cracked open the can and poured it equally between my old glass and his new one. He smiled at me and went back to his couch. 'That Coke is actually from Miles' shelf in the fridge. It's too much to hope that he won't notice it's gone. Ah, well.'

I couldn't think of what to say, so I settled for banality. 'Am I the first person you've told?' I asked. Thinking of Marjorie and Katherine and me on the beach this morning made me feel even more strange. Katherine suspected, but she didn't know, and it seemed to me that she ought to know, that her love for Nathan gave her first rights. Nathan somehow knew what I was thinking.

'No, I haven't told anyone else,' he said. 'Don't worry about Katherine. Not telling her has been almost as difficult as anything else I've had to deal with. Before I could handle anyone else's pain, I had to be able to handle my own. I've handled it, and now it's up to you all. Telling Katherine will be difficult for me because it will be so difficult for her. If I could, I would just disappear.' Nathan stared down at Odious, purring at the foot of the refrigerator. 'Tonight I'm feeling expansive and capable and you're here, so I said something. You're a good person to practise on, and much easier to talk to than Katherine will be. You will lose a friend, Katherine loses her "mate for life".'

I looked at him in surprise. In the midst of freakish,

stunning revelation it seemed odd that we would discuss matrimony.

'You know, now I can say that without being trans-fixed by the single male's aversion to permanence. I have no permanence left in my life. So I'm free to speculate on might-have-beens, and I'm free to take might-have-beens, like my marriage to Katherine, for granted.'

Listening to Nathan frightened me. Some part of my brain denied everything he said. But another, deeper, and colder part of my head said oh, yes, Nathan *is* dying. Believe it because you should have seen it coming long ago.

'Nathan, Miles has known for months that some-thing is wrong with you. I only learned that this morn-ing. I can't believe I haven't recognized the changes in you ... I'm talking too fast, aren't I?' Nathan nodded serenely and then we were quiet. Maybe some protective impulse inside my subconscious was trying to act on this even before I'd consciously accepted it.

'I can't think of anything all of a sudden, except that I shouldn't waste time with you, should speak fast, go fast, get everything I want to say in before you go.' Go, going, have gone, went; I conjugated the verb in my head. *Gone* is a more frightening word than dead. *Dead* doesn't mean a whole lot to live people. On hearing myself say gone, I felt my eyes fill and my throat close and tighten. I had a small hope that Nathan would tell me it wasn't true. Usually Nathan dispenses hugs like grandmothers dispense tissues. He just sat on his couch, though, and watched me compassionately.

'I know how you feel,' he said softly. 'It improves

if you let it. Man has an extraordinary capacity for blowing things all out of proportion. This is not a tragedy but an early departure. The tragedy would be if I were glad to go.' Nathan drank some Coke. 'I'm not,' he said simply.

Neither of us heard Penman come through the front door, but, as he approached the kitchen, his footsteps sounded very loud and out of context. Only seldom are the home fires burning when Penman returns, so his surprise at seeing Nathan and me awake was considerable.

Penman raised his eyebrows at us. 'Obviously, you all are waiting for the late late show, a three-thirty-five a.m. viewing of Bergman's *The Seventh Seal*. I shall watch this extraordinary opus while chewing rapturously on a mushroom omelette.' As Penman spoke he looked back and forth between Nathan and me.

'I seemed to have interrupted something momentous,' he said. 'Excuse me.'

Penman turned and left the room, but he was back even before his late night bar scent had reached us in the far corner of the kitchen. 'I could leave, or I could make enough mushroom omelette so that we might all partake.'

It was Nathan's decision, I thought, but all of a sudden, a mushroom omelette seemed like an outstanding idea. Crackers are all right for the night, but eggs cometh in the morning.

Nathan had a strange pained look on his face. I didn't think he wanted to talk about dying anymore, and yet he hadn't finished what he wanted to say. The look on his face reminded me of an expression I once found on Miles' visage, when, with all the bathrooms full, I had interrupted him mid-relieving himself out of the window. It was several minutes before Miles could begin again.

Nathan recovered more quickly. 'Well, I don't feel mentally expansive anymore, but I do feel like expanding physically, so if you'll make the omelette, Penman, I'll do the dishes.'

Penman pulled a package of brown eggs out of a grocery bag he'd brought in with him. Not a quarter mile from the house stands a huge all-night grocery store which only closes once every twenty-four hours for a fifteen-minute accounting session. We all use the store daily, delighting in the ability to pick up a pint of banana pudding ice-cream at five in the morning if we so desire. Penman in particular avails himself of the privilege of pre-dawn shopping, and his groceries are inevitably luxurious. Right after the brown eggs came fresh croissants, strawberries, a split of Laurent Perrier champagne, and a quart of newly squeezed orange juice. Nathan and I watched in astonishment.

'I feel I have made the right decision,' Nathan said.

After he cracked eight eggs into a bowl, Penman added grated Swiss cheese, two spoonfuls of sherry, and half of ten thinly sliced mushrooms. While he gourmeted at the counter, Nathan and I remained silent.

Clearing his throat, Penman said, 'whatever you were discussing probably had some tenuous tie to all the telephoning Nathan has been doing to the Medical College of Virginia. I bring this up because Katherine recently dissected the long distance bill. A number reappeared nine times to Richmond and she insisted it was mine. I rang the number to find out who answered at the other end. From dates and times of the calls, I deduced that the caller was Nathan. Why, my hairy and secretive friend, are you calling the oncology department at our estimable Virginia hospital?' Penman shook his whisk at Nathan and spattered drops all over the floor.

Nathan went to the counter to sample a mushroom. On the stove butter was beginning to sizzle in a frying pan, and the smell was rich. Calmly, Nathan looked at Penman and told him that he had pancreatic cancer and about three months to live. In the very best traditions of Southern emotional display, Penman fainted.

'Dear God,' Nathan said. We helped prop Penman up against the counter, and I waved some ammoniacal toilet cleaner under his nose.

'I'm torn between horror and humour,' said Nathan, looking almost as lost as I felt; it hadn't occurred to me that death had a deadline. Three months.

Penman lifted his eyelids gingerly and eyed Nathan, who began to smile. 'Are your corsets too tight? I've never seen anyone do that in real life,' he told Penman.

'And I've never been told one of my best friends has three months to live like that,' said Penman, retrieving his whisk.

'How many times have you been told a friend is dying? No one gives you instructions on how to tell your friends.' Nathan sounded rueful. 'I hate melodrama. I suppose I could have done this more traditionally. I could have dragged it out a long time and prefaced my remarks with "I'm afraid I have some bad news for you . . ." You both could have cried.'

My eyes prickled when he said that, and he shook his head at me. 'Remember. It's only sad if you haven't enjoyed the life you've had. Besides, if you cry, I'll probably cry too, and then, goddammit, my contact lenses won't work for days.'

'Are we the last to know?' asked Penman.

'No,' said Nathan shaking his hair. 'Just about the first. Not even my parents know yet. When I turned twenty-one I took over the responsibility for my health care, so no bills or notices have gone to them. All the bills come to me, and I send them on to my insurance company.'

'Nathan,' said Penman carefully. 'Far be it from me to question your discretion, but don't your parents and perhaps Katherine have a right to know? I mean . . .'

Shaking his head again, Nathan quietly interrupted Penman's hesitations. 'I haven't wanted to tell anyone. People say too much about dying. It makes it hard to finish living, and I have little enough life left that I can be selfish about how I'm going to finish it off. I want to do what I'm doing now. I want to be happy.'

For Nathan's sake I am not going to cry. What he's saying makes an enormous amount of sense. When I cry, I'll cry for me, and that will have to wait. For now I'll learn numbness. I don't know where to find the courage to match Nathan's, and I doubt I could be that brave if it were me dying. Strange to envy him now.

Penman seemed to be in conference with his conscience. Either that or he was trying to imagine what he would do in Nathan's situation. Whatever the reason, he was silent while he put the rest of the mushrooms and another fistful of cheese on top of the eggs, then flipped the yellow circle into a half-moon. He jiggled the pan a few times and then turned to face Nathan. Penman's eyes glittered wetly, but he smiled.

'In approximately thirty seconds, I shall offer you the worthy salute of my mushroom omelette.'

Smiling back at him, Nathan asked if he should pop the champagne. Penman deliberated a moment, and I could see him mentally dividing the small bottle between three glasses, then adding the orange juice.

'Well,' Penman said, 'if we use small glasses, then the ratio of wine to orange juice should be nearly palatable. Perhaps a bit weak, but still a worthwhile mimosa.' Nathan rolled his eyes and I picked through the strawberries.

Washing strawberries in warm water turns any time of the day or night into a temperate summer afternoon – just for a few moments with hands suspended above a colander filled with berries. I had a sudden feeling that if Nathan could eat enough strawberries, warm and droplet covered in a white bowl, he would live forever. I probably feel that way about all my favourite foods.

'Nathan, what do you most like to eat?' I asked.

He looked thoughtful. 'I have an Aunt Etty in El Paso, Texas who makes these outstanding black-eyed pea cakes which we eat with sour cream and salsa. That, I think, is my favourite food.'

'Oh,' I said.

'When I first learned that I was going to exit before I planned, I refused to believe it. Then I tried to cram everything in. All those protest marches last winter.

I had only a year, probably less if you count the time I'll be physically capable, to make my mark, to save everything I wanted to save. Driven like that, you tend to forget your original purposes. My goal became the justification of my own life rather than the plight of homeless people. Over the spring break I went to Texas to see Aunt Etty. I was there for a week, and we ate dozens of pea cakes and a gallon jar of her fiery salsa. I tried to eat enough to make up for all the black-eyed pea cakes I wouldn't have. One hundred pea cakes later, I hate them. But they are still my favourite food. I remember how the first one tasted.'

Penman ladled out our portions of omelette. After giving the strawberries an extra shake in the colander, I divided them between the three plates and put our powdered-sugar shaker on the table so that we could sweeten to taste. A basketful of croissants made a centrepiece. We all sat down, and Penman surveyed our fare with satisfaction. He chewed. Nathan examined a strawberry.

'Wouldn't it be odd if seeds covered our bodies?'

'It would certainly make the scattering of our seed a less clandestine operation,' Penman observed after a pause. I chuckled nastily before I could stop myself. Miles had just yesterday made a comment about all the possibilities Penman had for intrigue with Helen Wildly. Looking injured, Penman bit the middle out of a croissant.

'I'm ignoring you,' he told me pointedly. Nathan finally ate his strawberry.

Penman lifted his worthwhile mimosa and tilted it

slightly in Nathan's direction. 'A toast is somehow in order. To living as well as you can.'

Nathan and I raised our own glasses and we touched them gently to the others. I had a quick vision of a tippled twosome who drank together at The Raven's Roost on my Sunday night shift. All night the two had been toasting themselves and clinking their glasses with ever greater enthusiasm. Finally glass touched glass with such power that shards covered the table. Around our own table we were much more careful with our glasses and our toast. We acknowledged that glasses and life are equally fragile.

Nathan drank half his juice and then spoke. 'I realize there are probably questions that you have, and issues on which I need to elaborate. Explanations may come tomorrow. And a big favour to ask, all after I've told everyone.' He stopped to swallow and I saw his Adam's apple bob. 'Aren't you missing your movie, Penman?'

'That was certainly an abrupt u-turn in the conversation.' Penman took a dainty sip of his mimosa. 'Even Bergman isn't as absorbing as you are, Nathan. Besides, I timed my VCR to record it whether or not I was present to watch the film.'

Nodding, Nathan stood up and began to clear the table. My watch said three-fifty-five, so he had now been wearing his grey and red polyester pizza uniform for more than sixteen hours. Virtuously, it still looked fresh. I suppose perpetual freshness was the reason why our grandmothers got very excited over unnatural fibres when they were first invented. Nathan himself looked more rumpled. He had unbraided his hair when he got home, and now his face looked oddly small beneath that dishevelled mane. His eyes were sunk back in his head and had dark pouches under them.

'It's time to go to bed,' I said softly, when I realized Penman and I were both staring at Nathan. I stood and shook croissant crumbs off my bathrobe. 'Thank you for breakfast, Penman. Meeting the dawn will be difficult, but your warped eating schedule does have a perculiar charm. Nathan? Nathan!'

Nathan sort of collapsed back on the couch and I realized that I did not accept his dying, not at all. Certainly not right in front of my eyes. My heart hurt, and all of me felt full, too full to take another breath and maybe muster the control to say his name again. 'Nathan?'

'I'm very tired,' he said. 'Would you mind bringing me a blanket so I can sleep here? This is not a good time to disturb Katherine.' Nathan smiled faintly without opening his eyes.

Penman went to fetch the blanket, a stunning display of selfless servitude considering it was Penman. While my heart tried to beat normally again, I stood and watched Nathan fall asleep. Penman threw the blanket over him and Odious immediately went to settle in the warm canyon between Nathan's legs. All we could see of Nathan was some hair frizz and the back collar of his shirt, grey with red piping, so we turned out the lights and went upstairs.

On the landing, as I prepared to continue up and Penman to walk down to his closet, Penman had a question.

'Do you think he knew what we thought when he fell on the couch?'

'I don't know. I was afraid.'

I heard more than saw Penman in the dark. 'I don't think he was cognizant of our anxiety, as he may be unable to relate to that particular fear any longer. I feel certain he didn't mean to upset us. The tension in the kitchen was extraordinary, though.'

'You forgot the *chiaroscuro*, Penman.'

'What?'

'How can you analyse this like it's one of your movies?'

'That is not my intent. I'm attempting to think like Nathan,' he said.

Thinking like Nathan. 'Maybe that's what he meant about people interfering with his living. From now on I'll be watching him all the time, worrying. He's a different Nathan to me than the one I drove to work yesterday. If *I* feel that, what's Katherine going to be like?' I couldn't think anymore. It was too early, or I guess too late, and I was too tired.

'Good Morning, Penman,' I whispered and went up the attic stairs.

'Good Night,' he whispered in my direction. He started to say something else and I stopped climbing to listen. '"If you can keep your head when all about you are losing theirs and blaming it on you,"' he quoted. 'Kipling.'

The hall stayed quiet after that, but I was sure I could hear Penman smiling. 'Oh, Penman, you are an ass,' I whispered back, but I was smiling, too.

Though the moon was down nearly two moon-lengths from where it shone when I first went down-stairs, still the attic was bright with a pervasive moon fluorescence. Somewhere within me surprise registered. It seemed a very long time had passed since I woke from refried-bean-troubled slumber, yet Miles had not moved at all. He still huddled on his side with his legs sprawled in scissor-kick fashion. Putting both arms around him from behind, I nudged my face into his back. Less than thirty seconds later, my eyes closed in sleep.

The break of day went on without me. When I finally awoke, sunlight filled the attic, and individual shafts of light illuminated dust particles in stripes of dirty air. Miles wasn't in bed, which was initially puzzling, but then I remembered that he had to be in Washington by eight-thirty; he had probably risen and shone dimly shortly after I came to bed. It felt odd him not knowing about Nathan. But from what he told me yesterday, perhaps Nathan's news would be slightly less of a shock to him. How had Miles known? Did Nathan look any different?

The sun in the attic didn't feel like early sun. It felt like sun that has been around for a while and tested the air and warmed the wooden planks of the floor so that they feel alive to a bare foot. It felt like nine-thirty. I needed to get up and find a picture of Nathan from when he wasn't dying. No sooner had I chosen this course of action than footsteps began to climb to the attic. Marjorie appeared, tea mug in hand, in her elegant silk bathrobe and her fuzzy hair. She walked through two bright dust stripes and then settled on a chest at the foot of the bed. Her tea smelled of strawberries.

'We missed the sunrise,' she said, and tilted her cup so that she could blow on her tea before she sipped it.

'I slept right through my internal alarm,' I said, and she nodded.

'Penman came to talk to me early this morning. He woke me up and told me a Walt Whitman quote he had been trying to find. Walt said, "All goes onward and outward, nothing collapses, and to die is different from what anyone supposed, and luckier." I told him to go back to sleep, and he told me about Nathan.' Marjorie pulled her bathrobe around her. She looked small and fragile. She is beautiful and wealthy, and though philosophy has filled her thoughts with other people's pains, it has been by choice. Her own misfortunes have been few.

'No matter how I look at this, it is unjust. When I was small, I used to want to die to see what it would be like. Now dying makes me anxious. Ambrose Bierce said fear is a sense of the total depravity of the immediate future. I wasn't afraid until this morning.'

Instead of responding I leaned over, reaching under the bed to pull out a shoebox full of all the things I couldn't think of anywhere else to put. Marjorie didn't look up or move as I rifled through a stack of photographs from our years at college together. One picture of Nathan a year ago, at the start of our senior year, made me pause and catch my breath. How had we *not* noticed the changes?

In the photograph Nathan wore a tuxedo jacket with a bright orange velvet bow tie. The picture was mostly of his upper body, but Nathan's trousers just showed as jeans. His arm was around Katherine, who wore a white cocktail dress. Katherine appeared to be carrying a tumblerful of vodka jello, probably not her first of the evening. In contrast, Nathan seemed entirely sober, and his arm around her looked more utilitarian than proprietary.

The unusual thing about the picture should have been Nathan's notions of formal attire, but as I knew, jeans, orange bow ties, and a 1940s' black undertaker's coat were Nathan's choice of black-tie garb. Nathan once told me he had adopted this brand of elegance when he was eighteen; it was useful in discouraging Savannah, Georgia mothers from asking him to escort their debutante daughters to cotillion. The stunning point of the picture, however, was Nathan's face. His cheeks had curves and his eyes had firm tan flesh around them. I handed the photo to Marjorie and she set down her mug to bring the picture close to her face.

'He looks like what happens to a helium balloon as it gets old,' she said, shaking her head in denial. I knew she referred to a mental present-day picture of Nathan. She handed the photo back to me. 'He won't even have to tell his parents. They haven't seen him since June, at graduation. All they'll have to do is look at him.'

We both cried then, sitting in the dust-streaked sunny air. Tears feel wrong on hot dry cheeks. We cried for a long time. Once I got started, it was easy to keep crying. I just thought of the emptiness. It was easy to cry then for everything I'd miss when there was a hole in our house. Marjorie hugged me, which felt strange. Her contact with people is normally wholly mental.

Retreating back to her chest at the end of the bed, she handed me a tissue.

'Miles doesn't know yet, not for sure,' I said. 'He left for Washington early this morning.'

'He stopped by my room before he left. Penman was speaking very loudly and Miles wanted to know if everything was OK. Penman told him why it wasn't.'

'Oh.' All I could think of was Miles driving by himself, his suspicions confirmed. Whenever I have to cry, I do it in the car, so it was very easy to imagine Miles being sad, by himself, while he drove through quiet Virginia roads. The thought made my head hurt.

'Maybe it wasn't a good idea to tell Miles that right before he had a long drive by himself. He's not always the most careful driver anyway. How well is he going to drive when most of his head is back here with Nathan?' It was a relief to be angry rather than sad. I was glaring, now, directly into the window with its bright sun. My nose started to feel thick, up by the bridge, and I knew a sneeze was coming — a minor explosion. When I tried to look at Marjorie, much of her was obscured by big black sunspots and the little vein lines which are superimposed on eyelids after a colossal sneeze.

'Bless you,' said Marjorie. 'Penman drove up to D.C. with Miles.'

'You're kidding.' I didn't sound disbelieving on purpose, it just happened.

'Miles said he would be leaving Washington by early afternoon, so Penman decided he could go and be back for work at six. I think he was planning on sleeping at the Library of Congress while Miles toils.' Marjorie turned to look out of the window. 'You talked with Nathan last night,' she said to me via the window.

'Yes.' I stopped to consider what I wanted to say. 'I think that Nathan was trying to tell Penman and me that for him, the hardest part is done. When he talked about coming to terms with dying, it sounded like Ernest Hemingway writing of deep sea fishing: how you grapple with something and it tires you out and you tire it out and eventually you haul it in, having gained control, but somehow having lost anyway. It's probably not a very good analogy. I hate Hemingway. I don't know why I was thinking of fish when Nathan was talking about dying.'

'Winnie the Pooh, who is now revered as a popular philosopher, would say it was because you were hungry.' Marjorie turned from the window to look at me and she smiled so sadly that I wanted to cry again.

'What does Winnie the Pooh know? I'm just numb, I think.'

Marjorie's immaculate nails picked at the silk of her bathrobe. She must have chewed on them, because one jagged edge caught on the material and made a popping noise. Sometimes when my thoughts are wandering in too many directions, I focus my attention by filling my head with all the sounds of a particular moment. Picking nails, droning fan, sighing water, exhaling breath. The longer the silence, the more I hear.

'I'm thinking a lot more about me than I am about Nathan,' Marjorie said.

I thought for a moment before I replied. 'Dying is worse for the people who don't die. Dead people don't have to sit through their own memorials or funerals and they don't miss themselves afterwards. There aren't any holes in their lives.' Weirdly, an old tune sprung into my head – 'the worms crawl in, the worms crawl out . . .' Not big holes, anyway.

'Nathan sounds like he's getting a good deal out of this,' Marjorie said, and hugged her knees closer to her.

'I don't want it to sound like that. I guess I'm also thinking more of me than of Nathan, and I was trying to explain why.'

Marjorie unloosed her knees and walked to the far end of the attic. Without my contact lenses in, and at that great a distance, Marjorie resembled a large pink mushroom. 'I called in sick today,' she said. 'I need time by myself. To think.'

I nodded and remembered that Katherine and Nathan both had the day off today. Not by any special foresight, but because they always try to arrange their free days the same. Nathan told us last night that he would answer our questions today, so I guessed he would talk to us after Miles and Penman returned from Washington and before Penman and I went for our late shift at The Raven's Roost.

'Nathan said he had a favour to ask,' I said. Marjorie walked towards the stairs and transmogrified from a mushroom back into Marjorie. I saw her nod.

'Last night I made blueberry muffins for breakfast. Katherine and Nathan took a napkin with four of them out to the beach early this morning. I just heard them come back.' Marjorie started down the stairs. 'I require a nap in the sun, and I surmise that the sun has now warmed the world sufficiently. Would you care to come?' Marjorie's face looked tranquil once again, but her words gave her away. She spoke as Penman does, using *Penmantics*, as we called his speech patterns and word choices. Even Penman only talks like Penman because he's a little disturbed.

In the early afternoon, Katherine and Nathan came to lie on the sand with us. Marjorie remained oblivious to them for nearly half an hour, her head clapped between an advanced set of earphones that looked homely and like earmuffs. Her hands waved imperiously as she conducted an opera that I couldn't hear. I wrote letters and chortled at Marjorie. Katherine and Nathan just sat. Their faces had the destructive look of long tears.

'It's not getting as warm today, is it? The weather here is very unpredictable. Hot and cold like this lowers a body's resistance to germs.' Katherine frowned.

'Lie still, and as flat as you can – then the wind doesn't bother you and the sun has a chance.' I spoke with the authority my earlier gooseflesh gave me.

'It's an Indian winter. The locals at the Pizza Hut said that in early October a short chill would come, and then a short heat. After that, anything can happen. The guys said sometimes you'll get an eighty-five degree day, and then the next day an ice storm.' Nathan had a reference library of local lore in the teenagers who worked at his Pizza Hut.

'I imagine the water's warm; the weather was so hot yesterday. But today I haven't had the energy to walk down to the waves. Sunlight makes me complacent.' I stretched and yawned. It was very strange to try to talk normally. I felt like I did when I tidied the bed by pulling the blanket smoothly over rumpled sheets.

Nathan made some loud sucking noises and I looked over inquiringly. 'Want a piece of candy, little girl? It's a Lifesaver,' he said. I looked sharply at him, and he just looked back at me and smiled. Stifling a laugh, I thanked him and accepted the small, lime-green circlet with the ironic name.

Around five p.m. Miles and Penman drove up. I was in the kitchen, and though I couldn't hear the car, Odious jumped out of my lap and trotted to the front door. Penman's predilection for feeding Odious tins of smoked oysters ensures that Odious misses Penman when he's gone.

'Thanks, Penman,' I told him as he came in the door.

'Don't mention it,' he said, and gestured to Odious who sat at my feet and looked expectant. 'Are you both waiting for a tasty phlegmy titbit?'

'Thank you, no. Those oysters give the cat vile-smelling burps. Where is Miles?' I peered over Penman's shoulder. 'Are you both OK?'

'As much as can be expected. We are disturbed in spirit and somewhat weary about the coccyx bone. How're Nathan and Katherine?'

'About the same. Go away now so that I can give Miles a hug. My mother taught me never to display affection in public.'

'I have never in my life been referred to as the public,' he told me with great snootiness. 'Traffic coming in and out of Washington was ridiculous. I think I listened to Miles wish seventy-five times for diplomatic plates so he could speed down the breakdown lane with impunity.' Penman and his injured dignity headed into the house to find the others.

Miles was still out at the car organizing papers. I went out into the early evening and stuck my head through the window to say hello. In his discreet suit and tie Miles looked like new-printed money. When he stood up to hug me, though, I noticed the wrinkles which suits get after they've been in one position too long. Like fabric crows feet which emanate from the elbows, the backs of the knees, and either side of the crotch. I hugged him.

'Come on inside. Nathan wanted to talk to us this afternoon, and now is the only time we can all be here. I guess he wants to tell us all at once, rather than telling different things to each of us so we'd have to assemble it all.'

Miles nodded while I spoke. 'I don't really want to go in,' he said.

'It's strange, but I don't feel weird around him. I did at first, when I saw him this afternoon and he had been crying with Katherine. But you get used to it quickly. It's almost frightening how quickly you get used to it.'

Miles looked at me silently and didn't reply. I picked up his briefcase and went for the front porch. On the top step I turned and watched him. 'Come have a beer and some peanuts.'

He walked toward me and looked peevish. 'It's like retrieving a dog by rattling his biscuit box,' he said. He went past me into the house and I shut the door behind both of us.

The house smelled warm and spicy, like chicken curry. I went to don my electric blues. On the second floor landing, where I stopped to pick up a forlorn sock, I heard Penman rummaging around his room for his work clothes. By the time I was sartorially splendid in the approved Raven's Roost way, the upper floors of the house were silent.

Everyone was in the kitchen, and it took me a moment before I understood what was happening. The table had tiny squares of paper all over it — the notes we have left each other since coming to live at the beach. Rising from the middle of the table a candle loomed, taller and of a different colour than I remembered; suddenly I realized what activity involved my housemates. Ever since we arrived in Virginia Beach, a tall green candle has served as our message centre. Using pins to fasten bits of paper to the candle, we have slowly turned our wax kiosk into a shaggy fire hazard. Nathan seemed to have initiated the disrobing, and he was reading old notes and passing them around.

'"Anyone wishing to go to Busch Gardens next Tuesday, please volunteer to drive me there. I'll buy you *wurst* in the beer garden. Nathan,"' read Katherine. The note was written in scarlet crayon. I didn't need to see the paper to remember it. We had all rearranged our schedules so that we could go to Busch Gardens with Nathan. That was back in early August, and we had so much fun that we bought season tickets, even though the park would close at the end of October. Technically, Busch Gardens is an amusement park, but we go for the food, which follows the park's theme of a Europe that only exists if you believe in Camelot.

''We have ants,'' read Marjorie from another note written on the label from an insect repellent can. '''The little black dots in my raisin bread MOVE. Though I complained to the exterminator, he can't come until next week. Use the spray under the sink if you are likewise troubled. Katherine.'''

'Lovely,' said Miles. 'Here's one I like: "Penman, your mom called to say that Orphelia Van der Meer wants to have a luncheon to celebrate your latest magazine opus. Congratulations on belonging to a society which has raised LDL to an art form. Toodles, Nathan."'

'"LDL?"' I asked, coming to the table.

'Let's Do Lunch,' Penman said, looking both *tres* tired of his own sophisticated existence and haughtily astonished at having to explain himself.

'Penman,' I said, staring fixedly at his Raven's Roost shirt, 'the only thing which saves you from my nausea is the fact that your present attire entirely defeats the airs you affect.'

'If you are referring to my brilliant blue garb, I must say, along with dear Oscar Wilde, that I occasionally make up for being slightly under-dressed by being immensely over-educated.'

'Look at this one. How Miles,' said Katherine. The note referred to an emergency trip to the vet that Miles had taken with Odious. After she choked and drooled for the better part of an hour, Miles had scooped the cat into the car. The vet pumped Odious' stomach and the offending article was found to be a hairball. The trip cost Miles fifty dollars and he had been anxious to share the cost. The note listed everyone's contributions and detailed a total of twenty dollars and fourteen cents outstanding. Penman was listed as having offered eight dollars and eighty-six cents. Not surprisingly, Miles is the only one of us who faithfully balances his chequebook. Katherine is almost as scrupulous. But they both do this for different reasons. Katherine regulates her pink-plastic-with-geometric-designs chequebook so that she can create order in even that small sphere of her existence. Miles reconciles his worn black leather chequebook because he hopes to catch the bank cheating him.

If Penman and I didn't leave soon, we would be late. For Helen Wildly at The Raven's Roost, late was only marginally better than never. I wondered if Nathan didn't feel like talking anymore about death. At the table he was stacking all the little papers neatly. The notes were rumpled, and fit together loosely, like the leaves of pastry in a *millefeuille*. Then Nathan threw all the papers into the trashcan under the sink. I didn't want to leave the room yet, and I didn't want to prompt Nathan. Then I didn't have to, because he began to speak.

'My medical condition is not one I'm going to talk about very much, not because I'm being condescending but because it makes me tired to think of it. I have cancer and complications from diabetes. My body mutinied. Is mutinying. Apparently I have about three months before I abandon ship.' Nathan smiled a little as he sat down. The rest of us stood still, facing him. Nathan had sand stuck to his temple, where he had sweated and the wind had blown grains to settle and stick as though glued. Katherine noticed and made wiping away gestures which Nathan eventually understood to mean that he had a gritty forehead. He brushed the sand into his hair and kept on speaking.

'This is probably very strange to you. I am accustomed now to dying, but I wish it could be easier for you all. I have to go home for Thanksgiving, and I won't see you after that. That's part of the favour I want to ask. The rest of the favour is kind of weird. I want you to give me one day so I can say goodbye, not just to you, but to all of me.

'I want to have an extended flashback, like people have privately, in seconds, when they die suddenly. But I want to tell you my flashback and give you my memories, so you have all of me to remember. I do believe in life after death. I'm going to live in all of you.' Nathan's eyes were wide and he looked charged with purpose. As he spoke he leaned forward until his chin was parallel to the table. An electric silence hung in the air for a moment, then he relaxed back against the chair and humour creased his face.

'You all look scared to death.' He laughed, not meanly, but a great deep laugh. 'How does Friday, November the sixteenth sound? I don't normally plan things so far ahead, but this is a special case.' We all must have nodded, because Nathan still looked happy. Wrong. Nathan looked ecstatic.

'Don't worry,' he said. 'It's only as bad as you make up your mind it will be.'

Marjorie circled the table and gave Nathan her quick astonishing hug. She was smiling. And somehow, on our way to work, Penman and I smiled too.

Penman eased his great grey town car, one of his

father's discarded company vehicles, into the full service aisle of a Quik Stop gas station. The idea of automotive fumes on his fingers gives Penman the shivers, so he always pays someone else to pump the gas. He claims a person never recovers from the vulgarity of petroleum odours.

While the car was being filled up, Penman went inside the shop and returned with a pack of cigarettes and a Diet Coke. He handed the Diet Coke to me and cast a significant glance at the spread of my left thigh. I decided to ignore him. 'Well, I suppose I'll let Nathan live on in me.' Penman paused to draw elegantly on his cigarette. 'He'll have to cut his hair, though. I simply can't abide being furry.'

I wanted to laugh, but I was busy choking. 'Penman, will you please open your window? I am retching from smoke over here, even with my window all the way down.'

Penman cracked his window and we drove off, the brontosaurus belly of his car appeased at last with some twenty gallons of gasoline. All the way to The Raven's Roost the tape player played songs by a gravel-throated Tom Waits. I thought about memories.

5

Life went on. We all cried sometimes when we least expected to. I discovered that I produced particularly sticky saline tears which travelled down my cheeks in angry red lines. For the last part of September, my talks with Nathan made me uncomfortable; I felt sure that Nathan could see the track marks of my crying, and it was difficult to think of anything which seemed important enough to say. Already self-conscious, I was even more troubled to have to fumble for conversational topics with someone who used to precipitate in me a continuous patter. Though I will never understand how, one afternoon in early October the phone rang and sorted me out.

Marjorie and I were sitting on the back porch enjoying the day. It was a lovely autumn-coloured afternoon. As the summer heat and humidity went away, the beach had brightened. The moisture in the air had added fuzz to the shapes of things, and with that blurriness gone, everything looked sharper. A fountain of sea oats looked the very prototype of beach wheat. Individual pieces of sand lay defined on top of others. The sky was so blue that straight up it looked black, and the air made me feel like I was swimming in soft water. I was trying to read, but Marjorie had no other occupation than a circle of string which she had fashioned from her shoelace. After two pages of scanning words, I gave up any pretence of concentration and watched Marjorie try to make Jacob's Ladder out of her string.

'When I was at St Katherine's we'd do this at playtime. Anyone who knew the secret of Jacob's Ladder was forbidden to tell it to anyone else. I've forgotten it now. I got the secret from Emily Parke Simpson, who gave it to Penman after he agreed to kiss her.' Marjorie spoke absently.

Holding the backs of her hands to frame the string sculpture, she used the tips of her fingers to tangle and untangle, cross and re-cross. One string sculpture after another appeared and was re-formed. I unlaced my shoe and began to try as well. Just as we had all four hands stretched out to define two masterpieces, the telephone rang. No one else was home.

'Shit.' I still had my hands in the air.

Marjorie looked at me reproachfully and let her string drop. She picked up the phone in the kitchen, where I could see her clearly through the screen door.

'Yes. No. No. No . . . You're welcome.' Her monosyllables came at intervals, and the whole conversation lasted about two minutes. Then she hung up and I heard a sound like choking. I was startled enough to drop my string. Leaning forward in my chair, I peered through the screen door to see Marjorie hunched over the kitchen table. Her shoulders were shaking. I heard her gasp, and then again.

'Who was that?' My voice wavered even though I tried to control it. I *knew* the call concerned Nathan, and deep where my stomach knotted, I felt he was dead.

Marjorie shook her head and turned to face me with tears running down her cheeks. 'Oh,' she said, drawing a deep breath. And then I realized she was convulsed with her own odd brand of Marjorie mirth. So seldom have I seen her really laugh that I couldn't have recognized it. She pulled the hem of her shirt up to wipe her eyes, and finally, she looked at me.

'I feel sick,' she said, breathing hard.

It occurred to me that Marjorie had taken gentle, hyperventilating leave of her wits. But at the same time I was relieved. I wonder whether it's courageous or craven to believe the worst and then be prepared should it come. I was weak-kneed since it hadn't. Marjorie, for once less philosophical than I, began to hiccup. Interspersed with her maniacal teehees, the noise made me laugh, too. In seconds we were both laughing so hard that Marjorie was gripping the counter, and I was leaning on the door for support. Each time she hiccuped our laughter came anew. The humour of it was gale force, and it was all I could do to breathe out an important question. 'What's so funny?'

Marjorie took a gulp of air which combined with a hiccup so loud that it echoed. After the result-ant snorting laughter, she composed herself enough to speak.

'That was Kenilworth Cyrogenics. They freeze dead

people to reanimate them in a more benevolent age. As new customers, for this month only, we can register for their trial offer.' Marjorie began to laugh again, her hair quivering all over her head. 'For $100 a year they will freeze recently deceased pets up to the size of an Alsatian. Satisfaction guaranteed. The salesman was enthused about it. Last week he preserved his kitten.'

We whooped some more and the tears rolled down our cheeks. It felt so good to laugh that we laughed until we were exhausted.

'Stop, please, or I really will be ill,' I said, trying to get my breathing under control.

Marjorie, whom I have never seen actually grinning, nodded and came back to the porch. She picked up her string. 'I hurt,' she said.

'Think of some kid's poor frozen guinea pig. Do you think the rodent would recognize a more benevolent age if it faced one in its feed dish? The only way its life could improve would be if it could poop something that would be distinguishable from its food pellets.'

Marjorie looked perplexed. Perhaps the only pets in her household were Irish setters and horses. Calmer now, we listened to the rustle of the perfectly defined sea grasses.

'What will happen to Nathan's body, do you know?' Going back to my string, I laced the loop between the pinkies and thumbs of each hand. The question was more important to me than I wanted it to be, and I couldn't look at Marjorie. She had a nearly perfect Jacob's Ladder suspended in the air.

'He said he'd like to be useful. Whatever parts of him that still had a purpose should be recycled.'

I peered at my string, and I imagined discussing the alternative use of your own personal kidney at some time in the future when it could no longer process your own personal beer. Or your own cornea transmitting pictures to someone else's brain, even while it still showed *you* the tail end of a perfect fall day. 'What will happen after that, do you think?'

Marjorie answered softly, and I marvelled at the rapport that she, a ruminative, reserved, Southern whimsy, had with Nathan, who planned on leaving our lives as suddenly as a cliff drops off. She had talked with him about things which seemed so remote as to be untouchable. 'He'd like the remains to be burned and scattered, and a bench set in Seashore State Park. He's found that scattering is now illegal, along with every other form of litter, but we'll work around that.'

I looked across at her and saw her faint smile. 'The bench should say something,' I was thinking out loud.

'Nathan couldn't figure out the Latin for "We who have already bit the big one salute you". Then he considered, "Broad of butt and tired of feet, rest ye here in sweet retreat". He's not a poet. After that, everything was funny, like standing and reading greeting cards and losing all perspective of humour. "Here sat Nat whose life went splat." He finally settled on his name, and the dates, and the words "in memory of".'

'Does it worry you to talk to him about this?'

Marjorie was serene. 'No.'

'Do you think Nathan's death is actually real to you, or is it an existential possibility that you keep at a level where it can't touch you?' Though I wasn't trying to be mean, I was frustrated at her calm. *Dead* meant *gone*. I didn't think she understood.

Marjorie tucked her feet up under her and pulled her shirt over her knees. With the sun slanting away from our porch, the afternoon was cooler now. She finished weatherproofing herself by pulling her arms out of her sleeves. I was talking to a tepee with a head.

'"Is there any peace in ever climbing up the climbing wave",' she said. 'Tennyson, "The Lotus Eaters".'

'You know, Marjorie, not all of your quotes are immediately accessible to me. And I have to tell you, that is some serious bullshit coming from a person who looks like an advertisement for a pup tent.'

Marjorie gazed down the expanse of her shirt and sighed. 'Penman dislikes Tennyson, who I believe is more of a philosopher than a poet. I've been trying to broaden his horizons.' She puffed a breath of air down her shirt to warm her knees. 'Since Nathan has accepted dying, we have to. He isn't hopeless, just accepting. If we don't accept his acceptance, our defiance will destroy his peace as surely as it destroys our own.

'On some level, we feel sure that there is a cure which Nathan has not tried, or won't try, and we blame him. That's typical of our culture. All the psychological jingoism about stages for accepting death – the denial, anger, hopelessness stuff – applies only to Western civilization.' Marjorie retrieved an arm from inside her shirt and selected a strand of hair from her temple. She began to draw the hair repeatedly over her upper lip like a perpetual-motion moustache. I recognized the gesture. I've seen it when Marjorie is about to go farthest away, into the ether area of her brain where she expends most of her energy. Some absentminded human habit asserts itself to maintain a link with the physical surroundings her body can't escape. I think this earthly anchor must be common to highly intellectual beings. Perhaps Einstein picked his nose while unravelling relativity.

'Nathan's ideas draw from Hinduism, though that is probably inclination rather than education. He believes no end or beginning disrupts the universe, only a cycle of gradual decline and rebirth which is incorruptible and mirrors the travels of the soul. He will finish here and move again into existence. The body is merely a vehicle which wears down, necessitating a new one. These views may be only a panacea for dying men, but I believe in believing what works for you. Philosophy is finding out what works for you. Often, the people who come close to reaching a personal philosophy are called odd. Nathan has found a view of death which works for him, and we think it's strange.'

Marjorie paused, and I remembered her sitting in our college's lilac-walled café. Philosophy professors used to take her there for cups of insipid coffee. She was a bizarre sight in the dainty floral-patterned dresses her mother bought her. The pastel colours looked young for the age in her calm eyes. Our university was a small, friendly one, where professors and students often conversed together outside of classes. Some of the most important things I learned came from pleasant chatter with my professors. When Marjorie talked with the philosophy department, however, I had the feeling her instructors were learning from her. She was the only person they ever allowed to complete a full sentence.

As she spoke her animated moustache made me stare. 'Southerners in particular cherish their attitudes toward death. There's such opportunity for drama, no one likes to treat it simply. The prettiest building in a small Southern town is always the funeral parlour. Southerners do a technicolour, big-screen death in stage whispers. My mama says quietly behind her hand that her great-aunt has the *Big* C, or tells your mama at the country club that "it was her heart, you know". Then people excitedly tell everyone else. They develop facial expressions for grief which really mean oh-how-sad-let-me-run-tell-my-dearest-friend-Mary Elizabeth. And, convinced by all this drama, the dying Southerner – despite extraordinary suffering – puts more energy into staying alive another day than he ever put into *living*. It is possible and wise to just let go, but that's not a comfortable concept, and in the South, it's dismissed.'

I let Marjorie's words settle around me. There had been more of them in five minutes than I had heard, in total, in the past month. Any one of her statements would have frightened her staunch Baptist parents into spasms.

In the quiet of that peaceful day, I hoped that if I sat long enough, and tugged my earlobe or chewed my lip, I might become detached enough to think clearly. Hunger arrived before enlightenment, though, so I suggested that we go inside to make baked apples. Nathan came home from work while we waited for the apples to cook. To my relief I found I could speak to him more easily. I think the practical details of his death had been disturbing me, and it had helped to talk so openly with Marjorie.

'Can I tempt you with a slice?' asked Nathan, brandishing a cardboard box at me. It held another mistake, a thick, pan pizza creation of green pepper, ham, tomatoes, and pineapple.

'Easily tempted. I'm starving.' The aroma of greasy pizza filled the kitchen. I knew the leather seats of Marjorie's car, borrowed by Nathan for work, would smell of the juices which had permeated the box.

Nathan flopped on the kitchen couch and ate a slice of pizza. He looked awfully tired. His braid was still mainly intact, but there was an aureole of split ends around his face.

'Could be time for a trim,' I said, motioning to his mane.

He shook his head, smiling. 'I'm going to keep it while I can,' he said, and fished a stringy pineapple piece out from between his front teeth.

'My grandmother would question your breeding,' Marjorie said, eyeing the bit of fruit on his finger. 'Actually, Nathan, the gap between your front teeth would have made you a tremendously popular male prostitute in Chaucer's time. Gap-toothed people were thought to have unusual sexual prowess.' I leered at him.

'Katherine's been telling tales,' said Nathan. He examined the pineapple piece that lay on his finger and then ate it.

'Nasty. You know, Miles invariably picks his teeth after he eats. He's not afflicted with your suggestive gaping teeth, it's because his braces left spaces that act as food reservoirs. Last year for Christmas I gave him a retractable silver toothpick to fit on his keychain. I thought he could pick his teeth in style. Miles was disgusted; he said it was unsanitary, so he's never used the toothpick for anything more than tightening the tiny screws on his glasses.'

'If you ever decide you don't need Miles any longer, you should dust him off and give him to Katherine. I think they would make a very good couple.'

'Ugh.' I had a mental twinge when he said that. The idea made me uncomfortable either because I have always wondered whether Miles found Katherine attractive, however irritating, or because Nathan had referred to a time after he was dead. Mulling over this, I saw Marjorie looking at me.

'I told you he wanted to dispose of his useful parts,' she said. I must have looked puzzled.

'Kidneys, corneas, and Katherine,' Marjorie said. 'But Katherine and Miles wouldn't work, Nathan. They are too similar. Like two rival dog biscuit companies competing for the same market share in a tiny village in Ottawa.'

Both Nathan and I stared at Marjorie. What had come out of her mouth surprised even her.

'I've been reading James Joyce, and I need to counter him with large doses of reality to get perspective. Miles suggested I try Nathan's *Consumer Reports*. There was an interesting review of dog food in a back issue and . . . ' Marjorie decided to shut up. She looked sheepish, which I've never seen her do before. It was a matter of pursing her lips minutely and sliding her gaze off to the ceiling. Mentally I added *sheepish* to the small store of Marjorie's expressions.

Penman came down to the kitchen and demanded that I reveal to him the whereabouts of his boxer shorts. It was the day after Marjorie and I had talked about Nathan, and I was grating Parmesan cheese on popcorn. The kernels were hot, and I was trying to hurry so that the cheese could melt onto them. 'Come again, Penman?'

'Botheration. I am, or shall we say *was*, until a recent time, in possession of an exquisite pair of Egyptian cotton boxers which were made by my father's tailor in London.'

'How nice for you and your privates,' said Miles. He was waiting for the popcorn.

'Do you deny knowing about this?'

'Check Nathan's drawer, Penman. Katherine might have confiscated them for him when she was folding the laundry.' Miles waved him away.

Penman stomped out of the room.

'He has an unusual amount of energy for so early in the afternoon,' Miles said, retreating to the couch with a double handful of popcorn.

A moment later, Penman came back downstairs. All his bluster was gone. 'Where's Nathan?'

The tone of his voice made me look up from my cheese. 'What's wrong?'

'I couldn't locate my boxers because the door to Katherine and Nathan's room is locked on the inside. I believe Katherine is behind that door and refusing entry.'

Looking at Miles for confirmation, I said, 'I haven't seen her since yesterday evening.'

'Neither have I,' said Miles. 'Nathan took my car this morning to drive to Richmond for a check-up. He's staying overnight.'

'Let's leave Katherine alone for a while,' I told them. 'I know she and Nathan had a fight yesterday. She said she couldn't speak to his parents again, knowing that they didn't know that Nathan was dying. It ended with her slamming the door of their room. Nathan had to sleep on the couch last night.'

Penman nodded. 'I myself have done that on occasion, but never in ire, usually in torpid slothfulness. Do you think Katherine has remained up there ever since?'

I didn't know. 'Give her some time. This is rougher on her than on anyone else.'

Miles seemed to have accepted Nathan's dying, and he had little patience for Katherine's tempers. Cramming a palm of popcorn into his mouth, he dusted his hands on his shorts. 'I'll loan you a pair of my fine boxers, Penman. They're lovely, 100 per cent South Carolina cotton, discovered by me in a pile of unclaimed property in the laundry room back at college.'

Penman snorted. 'I am grateful, certainly, but I would sooner free-ball it.'

I went by Katherine's room several times. Though I stopped and listened, I heard nothing. But she had to be in there; she wasn't anywhere else. Later, I had proof she was there, because I picked up the phone and heard her voice. She must have used the extension in her bedroom. I said, 'sorry,' and put the phone down immediately. It occurred to me, since I had heard no sounds of her getting ready for work, that she was calling in sick. I decided to knock on her door.

'Katherine. It's me. Do you want anything to eat?'

'No.' Her voice was muffled and tear-filled. 'Please go away.'

I started to speak again, but I didn't know what to say. Standing two inches away from a locked door that you know won't open was a humbling experience. I went away disliking it. We needed to make allowances for Katherine. Coming to terms with Nathan's death was hardest for her. By nature she is least inclined to simply accept. Since she first learned of his impending departure, she has denied it, often angrily. Retreating was a strange step for her, and I was worried. The reasoned Katherine I knew would not refuse to come out of her room.

We didn't see her until Nathan returned from Richmond the next day. She walked into the kitchen just as he and Marjorie were celebrating over his news.

'I won't have to lose my hair,' said Nathan exuberantly.

'You'd have looked like a bald bear,' said Marjorie, after gazing at him intently. Neither of them noticed Katherine's foul humour.

Nathan cut a lock of his hair and tried to put it into a locket around Katherine's throat.

'I don't think this is funny,' said Katherine. She hit his hand away from her neck and glared at him. Her nostrils were flared like they are when she is very angry, and I had a quick vision of Katherine as a child, furious because someone mixed the red and yellow modelling clays together.

Nathan looked at her and he made me feel lonely. 'It's not my fault, Katherine. But I could hate you if you don't let me do this my own way.' He stared at her for a few seconds more, and then he went out to the beach.

'Goddammit.' Swiftly Katherine bent for our message candle on the kitchen table. I barely had time to see it smash against the door frame and break reluctantly, the wax tearing apart messily. The string of the wick held the big pieces together, but we would have wax flecks on our toes for days.

'Goddammit,' Katherine sat down at the kitchen table and started to cry. 'It's not like he says. He treats it like some mystical thing that's happening to someone else. It's not easy, and it's serious. Humans don't just get sick and then leave, like you leave school or a restaurant. Dying isn't leaving, it's dying. How can he talk about it like he does, like it doesn't matter? I want to know what's happening. I can't understand it. Maybe he's just giving up. Maybe he could be helped. I know enough medicine so I could understand what's wrong. But I can't just let this happen.'

Neither Marjorie nor I could say anything; we didn't know what to say. Maybe Nathan *was* making it difficult for Katherine. He'd had nine months to accept his death. Katherine had had just one and a quarter. I sat down on one side of Katherine while Marjorie went for a box of tissues. Then Marjorie decided that we needed some tea. She left me at the table with Katherine.

'Oh dear.' I sighed before I could stop myself, and Katherine looked blearily at me.

'Why's it so simple for you?' Her tone was resentful.

'I guess I love him differently. He's my friend, not my boyfriend. Maybe it's easier to act like he does because I'm not attached like you are.' Even while I spoke I knew that only part of what I was saying was true.

'You are all more like Nathan than I am.' Katherine began to cry again. 'Usually I'm thankful for that, because he's not very sensible. But it's a barrier now.' She cried with her fist pressed into her cheek, and it hurt horribly to watch her. Katherine had found something she couldn't nag into compliance. Death doesn't care if it's unhygienic or untimely.

Marjorie set a mug in front of Katherine. 'Let it steep. You and Nathan would have made a good pair. It's good that you're different. You complete each other's inconsistencies. That makes this harder now, though.'

Marjorie paused to think and sip. 'Love. You have to love him enough to want to make it easiest for him. If you can love him like that, then you'll forget about you. It'll be easier for you. If you remember how he handles dying for the rest of your life, then you'll remember and love Nathan forever. And it'll only hurt a little.' Marjorie looked exhausted, then, and her eyelids fell shut. I think words make her tired because she cares about them too much.

We all sat and sipped our tea. I needed a tissue. Probably just to wipe away my mug's steam, where it condensed on the area around my eyes.

When Nathan came back from the beach, Katherine

and Marjorie and I were still sitting around the table. Nathan brought the smell of wind and salt in with him, and the smell gave us more energy. And an appetite. Marjorie and I decided to find food. We went out to the grocery store, leaving Nathan rubbing Katherine's cheek. Ours was a tactful departure.

'Marjorie,' I asked her as we walked down the street, 'do you love Penman?'

Marjorie stopped trying to blow a whistle into a blade of grass and looked at me. 'Yes.'

'Would you ever marry Penman?'

Marjorie went back to working on her blade of grass. I assumed she was thinking over the question. She took too long. Though she made me feel that I trespassed on sacred ground, the urge to hound her possessed me.

'This can't be the first time you've thought of this. If he married anyone else, how would she be able to understand about your friendship? Or, even more complex, how would any man you married be able to accept Penman? Or else, scary thought, think of any children you and Penman might produce. They'd be languid, albino philosophers with ancient souls at birth. I'd be an excellent aunt to send them to when you needed a vacation.' I was getting interested in this idea. Being an aunt would be almost as jolly as being a grandmother, better in fact. I'd never have to go through any maternity hassle myself.

'Shriek.' Marjorie finally produced a noise from her blade of grass. I had a sense that, having got that out of the way, she could now deal with issues of lesser importance. 'You're nearly as bad as my mother. She has been planning my wedding to Penman for twenty years, and she wishes I were half as interested in "catching" Penman as I am in "dead people who had queer thoughts".' Marjorie mimicked her mother's aristocratic drawl.

We were at the store's entrance, now, and the electric eye courteously opened the door for us. We walked in, pausing only to gather up a grocery basket. 'I'd like to make caramel apples,' said Marjorie. She stood at the produce display and selected six apples, avoiding those with bruises and spots. Before she came to the beach, she thought all apples were the perfect, tissue-wrapped ones her family had shipped from Washington State.

'Gee, Marjorie,' I said in my finest North Carolina drawl. 'You're gonna make some fellow a fine little housewife some day.'

Expressionless, she stared back at me. 'May you choke on fried pork rind. Penman and I have given each other the right of first refusal. That, of course, was the way Penman worded it.' As if I wouldn't have known that.

We took our purchases back home. I had wanted to buy everything, but I settled, finally, on a pineapple and the makings of gingerbread. The temperature was about fifty-five degrees and it was a fine fall day. The time was ripe for gingerbread.

'My trust fund for a manservant.' Penman took his hand from the rake's handle to peer with disbelief at a possible blister.

'It is my belief, Lord Fauntleroy, that manual labour is tonic for the soul,' said Nathan, who was looking very thin with his shirt off.

We were spending the day at Miss Alice Rose Cromwell's Singing Pines, where the task at hand was raking away the pine needles which completely covered Miss Alice Rose's wilful front lawn. A few days earlier, Miss Alice Rose had called to ask if we might give her a hand with some yardwork. Her 'damn fool man', she said, had tripped on the porch stairs and dislocated his hip. He normally dealt with the pine needles, but, as he could not, she wondered if we would be willing to help out.

After consulting us all, Marjorie had settled on this afternoon because we could all come. Even Penman had agreed to rise before noon so he could make the trip out to Singing Pines. He hadn't planned, however, on doing any actual work; rather, he thought he might have a diverting chat with Singing Pines' spirited chatelaine. But Miss Alice Rose possessed six rakes and an indomitable will which crushed Penman's determination to sit on the porch with a fresh lemonade.

The pine needles smelled warm and resinous in the sun. Marjorie called them 'tags'. For her the slim brown nuisances were a fond childhood memory.

'On autumn weekends Daddy used to direct the gardener to rake up the pine needles as soon as they fell. Grass turns yellow quickly beneath pine tags. Wheelbarrow-loads of tags came back to my play corner, and I'd heap them into walls. Once a six-foot wall collapsed on Penman, and he smelled like a Christmas tree all weekend.'

'Marjorie,' Penman said, 'if I remember rightly, you had reprehensible notions of what the rooms in your pine tag château should be called. I recollect one disagreeable occasion when you used pine tags to block out an eight-room edifice, and you didn't even delineate an area for the butler's pantry. I never told your parents. They would have required you to do a punitive summer session of charm school. Dear God. I believe I'm sweating.'

Miss Alice Rose descended from her porch steps and approached us. She was wearing the same bathing suit she'd worn when I first met her, and she carried a stack of folded bedsheets. 'Why, you all are coming along real fine. I brought some linens to rake the tags onto. Then you can bundle the beasts back into my compost pile. I thought we might break for a spell around two, and I can feed you all a bit of lunch. It's the least I can do.'

Katherine thanked her for all of us, and she watched Miss Alice Rose go back inside. She was enchanted with Singing Pines. I'd been afraid she'd deem it a health risk, so Marjorie and I had avoided bringing her on any of our previous visits to see Miss Alice Rose.

'This is unusually attractive for a place whose building materials look less reliable than playing cards,' Katherine said, squinting at the house through the sun. And Miss Alice Rose had taken immediately to Katherine, too. She insisted on squiring Katherine and Nathan about through the house. While Katherine and Nathan partook of the grand gander, Miles, Marjorie, Penman, and I surveyed what we had gotten ourselves into.

'I didn't remember the front yard as being so large,' said Miles grimly.

'Many hands,' I began, wagging my finger at him.

Penman interrupted me. '. . . May shirk work.' But he wasn't allowed to.

Shortly before our designated lunch break we finished the front lawn. Each of us had taken a section and scraped piles of pine needles, and the piles had gradually consolidated into bigger piles. It became a game to see whose pile could consume the most little piles. Nathan, his weedy body covered with sweat and clinging pine bits, won the contest. With sweeping strokes of his rake, he rolled the small piles into his monster mound. Marjorie made a brave attempt to foil his onslaught by raking close to his mountain and trying to snatch a chunk of it. In her haste, she seemed to be performing a graceful rake dance. I wondered aloud if she had learned that at cotillion.

Marjorie didn't hear me. '"Half a league, half a league, half a league onward,"' she cried.

Leaning on his rake to watch, Penman said, 'Even if I could reconcile myself to Tennyson, I could never be bothered with "The Charge of the Light Brigade".'

'"Mine not to make reply,"' called Marjorie breathlessly. She changed her tactic as Nathan noticed her efforts and charged at her with rake held high. Throwing her own rake aside, she tumbled into Nathan's pine needles. Miles shouted happily, running to leap in, and Nathan followed. Soon the pile was scattered.

Katherine made spitting noises from where she had collapsed on the edge of the pile. 'I think I swallowed a spider.' She screwed up her face and I snapped a photograph. I'd brought a pocket camera, figuring that this day should be recorded tangibly. Then I photographed Penman and Nathan frantically trying to cover Miles in pine needles.

Guiltily, we gathered the far flung pile onto Miss Alice Rose's bed linens. Working three to a sheet, we scuttled loads of pine needles back to the barely distinguishable compost heap. Just as we finished Miss Alice Rose called us to lunch. Standing by the front door she rang a porcelain dinner bell.

'Time to wash up,' she said.

We all took turns at her big kitchen sink. She had black soap which smelled exquisite, and when I finished sniffing that, I smelled the air. I suppose I had been expecting ham, biscuits and potato salad, but the odours in the room belied traditional Virginia fare; indeed, the air shimmered almost brown with the scent of curry. On the kitchen table Miss Alice Rose had set seven bamboo trays, and on each tray sat five small bowls.

'Like Indian food?' asked Miss Alice Rose. 'I love it. Learned to eat it when my older brother dragged me kicking and screamin' out to the Punjab in 1933. He got all the way out there and expected to eat field peas and country ham, was real upset when he couldn't. But I took to native food and watched the servants cook it. Ever since I find myself bored to tears by Southern cooking. My mama is thrashin' in her grave, I expect.' As she spoke, Miss Alice Rose filled the bowls on all the trays. Some of the food steamed with a pungent fragrance that made my nose twitch. Miss Alice Rose noticed.

'You look like a rabbit. The spice that set you wondering is coriander. I grow it in my garden and it makes the cats wild. The Indians use it like we use parsley. We're going to eat *thali* style,' she continued, ladling a pale creamy mixture into one bowl on each tray. 'That means that everyone has everything they need for the whole meal on one tray. No interrupting, no passing. Much more civilized. Now everyone take a tray and come with me out to the back porch. I've got a pitcher of iced tea out there.'

Rather stunned, we trundled off after Miss Alice Rose. She had pulled up chairs and a bench around a coffee table. The porch was bare, otherwise, and it had an excellent view of the water beyond her overgrown back garden.

'Miss Alice Rose, would you be offended if I asked what's in each dish?' Katherine wore her wide-eyed courteous look. I hoped she wasn't going to begin lecturing about the adverse effects of strong spices on elderly stomachs.

Miss Alice Rose, who was pouring glasses of iced tea and garnishing them with mint sprigs, shook her head. 'Why certainly. I bet none of this is what you'd expect. This here', she pointed to an orange and green combination, 'is papaya and pepper salad. I guess you might call it the first course. Over here we have saffron pilaff. This', she gestured at a dish of bright pink chunks, 'is tandoori chicken, baked in a clay oven. That next to it is cauliflower with ginger, and beside that, yoghurt salad with mint and roasted peppers. The little bowl with relishes in it has tomato and plum chutney and coconut chutney. I make those myself. At Christmas time I put my chutneys up in pretty jars and send them to folks. All the people who were expecting my mother's secret recipe strawberry preserves, which everyone in Charleston has thrown away for years, are pleasantly surprised. Mama, you see, could not taste a thing, and most years she put so much lemon in her conserves that one spoonful would sour your whole day. Well, what are you waiting for? Eat up!'

Miles had already finished his papayas and peppers and was scooping into his yoghurt salad. 'This is excellent, Miss Alice Rose.'

Miss Alice Rose beamed at him. She looked to me like an exceedingly lively dried fruit with her dark tanned skin and wizened face.

'And what prompted your brother to journey to India in 1933?' asked Penman.

'It was his mind. The men of my family have always been a bit soft in the head. My Daddy shot himself in 1925 when a fox turned on his favourite Jack Russell and ate him. Daddy just couldn't live it down. That dog had been siring champion foxers for years, and it was just too humiliating that his old dog got beat up by a fox. So Daddy killed himself. Mama wouldn't have Daddy buried in consecrated ground 'cause she said that a man who had no more sense than a junebug couldn't rest with decent people. It was a scandal. But the women in my family have always been like that. Anyway, Mama was so disheartened she passed away soon after. I was left to my brother.'

'He was a deal older than I was and he had been at loose ends since the end of the war. He'd tried takin' over my Daddy's ailin' tobacco business, but that didn't work and after about ten years, all my Daddy's old friends got tired of giving Ellesmere jobs. So he took it into his head to bring the pleasures of being a Baptist to some heathen peoples. He wanted to tell those folks who worshipped cows a thing or two, so we set off to India. Old Ellesmere took me along because I was set to make an unsuitable attachment. All of Charleston was talking about me, and Ellesmere thought he owed it to the family name to stop the waggin' tongues. We were out there ten years, and I loved it once I got there.' She stopped to nibble at a piece of tandoori chicken.

'Was your missionary work successful?' Nathan looked wistful as he spoke. He had wanted to make a difference in someone's life. Even though his fervour didn't go on religious lines, Nathan understood Ellesmere's need to crusade.

'Oh, Ellesmere got a couple of people excited about the communion wine, but that was about it. After a while he turned Hindu on me, and I decided to come home.'

I heard a sound suspiciously like Penman suppressing a snort. It made chewing his cauliflower very difficult. While I watched Penman, Miles took my last piece of chicken.

'You all don't talk much. Guess that's why lunch went so quick. If you boys are finished, would you mind stepping out to the dock and pulling my crab pots up for the winter? We ladies are goin' to have a toes up and watch you.'

Setting aside their trays obediently, Miles, Penman, and Nathan went out of the back door and began picking their careful way to the dock about fifty yards away.

'Well trained, your young men are.'

'Not really,' said Katherine. Miss Alice Rose looked at her sharply.

'When did you come to Singing Pines?' asked Marjorie.

'Singing Pines belonged to my Mama, and she left it to me. My unsavoury attachment waited for me while I was in India. When I returned in 1943, I married him and brought him here. The good people of Charleston wouldn't have been tolerant of a mixed marriage between one of their own and a hired hand. Even here I had to keep my maiden name.' Miss Alice Rose's eyes sparkled at us.

'I was naturally dark-complexioned, and soon after Neville and I came to Singing Pines the sun made my skin so brown people thought I was black. It made things easier.' Miss Alice Rose stretched her feet out to rest on the coffee table. 'In 1965 Neville passed away and I've been here ever since. *Cancer.*' She whispered the last word. I felt Marjorie's eyes settle on me significantly.

'It's nice to have somebody to pull those crab pots out for me. Would you girls give me a hand with the dishes?'

In the kitchen Marjorie and Miss Alice Rose washed and swapped debutante stories while Katherine and I dried and listened.

'I looked like a roll of commode paper in my ball dress,' said Marjorie. 'Not a vision of loveliness. After I did the promenade, Penman and I took off our shoes and went running on the golf course. It was a dry summer that year, and even the grass on the putting greens felt like straw.'

'Well,' said Miss Alice Rose, 'I was presented in Birmingham *and* Charleston, and the men lined up to escort me. Those were grand times. The clothes for my debut in Birmingham took up eight trunks. I was so busy lookin' dainty at functions I never thought to eat. My Mama had to bring her dressmaker down to take my dresses in emergency-like. I'd lost two inches from my waist and my bust'd shrunk pitifully.' Miss Alice Rose shook her head as she remembered catastrophe. 'How long did your season last?' she asked Marjorie.

Marjorie smiled. 'As long as my dress did. My mama took me home midway through the ball because I'd smeared my gown with grass stains. All the other debs were impressed – they thought I'd done something illicit in the Country Club bushes. I became a legend that night. Mama knew better. She figured Penman and I had been rolling down hills on the fairway.'

Katherine sucked in Marjorie's words, and watching her listen, I laughed to myself. I was sure Marjorie had just added something somehow to Katherine's fixation with Penman and Marjorie's sexual relations. I should say lack thereof.

I wonder why Marjorie's tales of upper-crust Southern pageantry don't make me cringe the way Penman's do. In his acceptance speech for the Nobel Prize for Literature, William Faulkner discussed the difference between 'survive' and 'prevail'. Marjorie knew the speech by heart, and she had recited it for me one night when I made a raid for gingerbread. Faulkner was one of Marjorie's gods. I thought the difference between 'prevail' and 'revel', while less subtle, was more important. Penman revelled in his upbringing and it made my stomach queasy. Marjorie had prevailed over hers, and it made me chuckle.

'Doesn't the concept of "coming out" – and being a debutante – just encourage women to think that they are only present for the pleasure of men?' Katherine somehow managed to look condescending while waving her dishtowel.

Miss Alice Rose laughed. 'Honey, let me give your neck a hug. Why of course it's hard for you to understand. All those goose-brained Oprah Winfrey women have muddled your head. Coquetry, flirtation, and dressin' up nice – that's not for the pleasure of men, that's for the pleasure of *you*. Hush now, look who's coming. Hello, boys. We were just havin' a chat.'

It was time to take our leave. Penman and I had to be at The Raven's Roost by five-thirty p.m. Miles commented as we walked out that Miss Alice Rose's backyard might need a hand in the spring. She was grateful.

'I'll do a lunch for you again, and you can sail if I rummage around and find a rudder for the little dinghy. Singing Pines and I will be right here.'

His key poised to unlock the passenger side of his car, Miles discovered that Marjorie had never locked it. 'You were the last one out of the car, Marjorie, and you didn't lock it.' Miles' tone was accusatory. On Marjorie's car all the doors lock centrally, and she occasionally forgets that other automobiles are not so conveniently equipped.

But Miss Alice Rose had brought out a side of Marjorie that Miles could have done without. Placing her hands firmly on her hips, she said, 'City boy, Northern thing, what are you locking for out here?'

'Habit,' Miles said. 'This is America.'

'Miles,' declared Marjorie, 'you are American by birth, but an American can only be Southern by the Grace of God.'

Miles merely looked disgusted. It was Penman who made reply. 'How extraordinarily squalid,' he said. 'I gather, Marjorie, that you have been perusing key rings in South Carolina truckstops.'

Piling into the car, Penman, Miles, Marjorie, and Nathan jibbed each other in friendly fashion. I stopped paying attention to them when I turned to see Miss Alice Rose murmur something to Katherine on the front porch. On tiptoe, Miss Alice Rose stood with one hand on Katherine's shoulder. Tilting her head down to catch Miss Alice Rose's words, Katherine suddenly stepped away. The two talked a moment longer. I saw Katherine nod and wipe at her eyes. As she started toward the car I intercepted her. Though she looked stricken, she turned with me to wave at Miss Alice Rose.

'She told me to look after my young man.'

'Oh, Katherine. I'm sorry.'

'She said he looked too skinny, and she has seen people look that way before. He'll be in her prayers, she told me.' Katherine sniffed quietly and rubbed hard at her eyes.

We crushed into the back of the car, and Nathan looked concerned as he saw Katherine's face. She smiled at him. 'It's hay fever. I really think it clogs the respiratory system to do yard work without a protective mask. I hope you all remember that next time.'

If next time were spring, there would only be five of us.

We all wanted to spend time with Nathan, and I feared we were beginning to infringe on his privacy. He got very irritable with me one morning when I insisted he come to a pumpkin patch with me. Full of Halloween spirit, I wanted him to come along to smash the black widow spiders which dependably lived on the underbellies of pumpkins.

Nathan declined. He lay on the couch with newly arrived issues of *The Economist, Soldier of Fortune*, and *The New Yorker*. 'I need some peace, and I want to catch up on my periodicals. Penman has an essay on oatmeal in *The New Yorker*. I haven't had a chance to read it.'

That should have been enough, but I persisted. 'Come on. I never get to see you. Besides, I want a huge pumpkin, and I'll need help carrying it. Don't be a blob.'

Nathan just looked at me.

All of us except Miles have cut back at least one day on our work schedules. There is a need, when living with a dying person, to see him constantly. I had the feeling we were trying to stock up on Nathan, to lay in a supply of his character that would never run out. And as long as we saw him often, we knew he was still there. I thought abandonment was an emotion felt only by children who lost their parents. Learning otherwise frightened me.

We were laying a heavy burden on Nathan, who liked a regular dose of solitude. Though Miles could not cut back to a four-day week, he went surfing every morning with Nathan; Miles had managed to re-arrange his work day so that he could arrive later and leave earlier. Childishly, I was slightly annoyed that he hadn't bothered to do this for me. But I don't think Nathan appreciated the effort. Nathan had taken to hiding, like kittens do when they are played with too often. My feelings were hurt, but I understood, when I saw Nathan slip out of the house and settle behind a large clump of sea oats. I left him there to read his magazines.

'White Rabbit Day.' I said it quietly to myself before saying good morning to Odious. It was the first of November. The days were getting shorter and I found I valued early morning even more. No matter how early we arose in summer, there were always people on the beach. Now at dawn we have the beach to ourselves. I often go out before Marjorie, Nathan, or Katherine, because the winter water is best appreciated alone. Though the rest of Virginia Beach wallowed in late autumn, down by the water it was cold. The seashore itself has only two seasons, and when it's not summer, it's winter.

The summer beach brings out vanities: people tanning; teenagers wearing minimal bathing costumes and hoping to be noticed by others; part-time surfers who believe they can conquer waves. Lonely and grey, huge and crashing despite lack of an audience, the winter waves made no concessions to humanity.

I feel insignificant out on the cold sand. Aeons before I began life, and long after I leave it, the ocean will continue to roll here, foaming and frothing as it finally meets a boundary.

One very early morning, as I tried to lace my sneakers around feet made fat by an extra pair of socks, I looked up to find Nathan, dressed for the beach. He was surprised to see me.

'I wanted the beach to myself, but I think I'm too late,' he said.

'I could make tea before I go out, Nathan, and then you'd have a few minutes by yourself.'

'Thanks.'

He was back before my tea finished steeping. 'My fingers are blue. I don't think my blood circulates as fast as it used to.'

'My grandfather says that, but he's eighty-three.'

'Yes, well, we've all got our reasons.' Nathan went to the stove to warm his fingers. When he turned to face me, I saw questions in his eyes. 'If you look back,' he said, 'what actual *moments* stand out in your life? I don't mean what was most important — like college graduation or your twenty-first birthday. Pretend your memories are like a crowd watching football. If you blur your vision and let your eyes sweep the crowd, some colour or person draws your attention. Look at your memories like that, and tell me which ones pop out.'

'Oh, Nathan, I don't know.' I tried to think as he'd directed. 'The first thing that comes to mind happened when I was seven. My kitten had disappeared a week earlier, and I called for it every night. My parents would put me to bed, and after they fell asleep, I'd get up to call again. One rainy night, the kitten came back.' I spoke slowly, remembering the wet cement, cold on my bare feet, and the kitten, coming towards me with fur slacked down by the rain and tail high in the air.

'Does anything else stand out?' he wanted to know.

'Why are you asking?'

'Because I'm trying to decide what to tell you all when I have my verbal flashback on the sixteenth of November. You haven't forgotten, have you?'

I hadn't forgotten about our promise to reserve a day for Nathan to say goodbye. We often speculated on what he was planning.

Nathan pulled his hair over his forehead and looked at me through it. Barely able, now, to see his face, I felt like curtains needed to rise from the stage. 'I've been around Katherine too long,' said Nathan, 'I'm beginning to have "theories". The flashbacks that people have in the split seconds before they fall, or before they see a car smash into them, are fascinating. Most people don't live to tell them, so I don't know as much about them as I'd like to, but the general consensus is that people see brief images of the significant events in their lives. I've been trying to determine what is actually important to people. In my own case, I know it's not big events that stand out, but faces, and episodes like you calling your cat. My flashback might also include regrets. Things I wish I'd done, but never had the time. Like parasailing, and learning to play the banjo. My theory is that most people would be surprised at the seeming insignificance of the images which occur to them right before they die.'

'I think I'm in over my head, Nathan. If you want someone to add insight to this, you'd better speak to Marjorie.' Sometimes the things I'd like to say are too difficult to articulate, so I stay quiet. What I wanted to say was that my ideas about life were changing, and that maybe the brain reverted to its innate wisdom in the moments before a violent death. The brain recognized that the important things of existence often pass daily without fanfare. Right before dying, the brain tries to arrange for enlightenment.

Nathan watched me think. 'Let's see if the sun is up yet. My colleagues at the Pizza Hut tell me dawn is just the right time to check the day's weather. "Dawn is ideal," a pizza cook told me, but I think he might have been referring to his girlfriend.'

It was the start of the second week in November before Nathan finally quit the Pizza Hut. As a tribute when he left, his adolescent co-workers raised upon a pizza crust a mountainous tower of all the strangest ingredients they could imagine. Nathan brought his pizza trophy home and we admired the artistic nests of anchovies filled with pine nuts, sweetcorn, pineapple, and croutons. Odious enjoyed the anchovies.

The teenagers at the Pizza Hut had made Nathan a minor deity. They christened him Matt Nat, because he never glistened with sweat when they were all working around the pizza ovens. Most of Nathan's colleagues were the proverbial surfer dudes who saw the last year of school as a monstrous impediment to big waves. Pizza Hut became a part of their creed when their ringleader, Edward Kin, got a job as a dough maker. Edward got jobs at the Hut for all his friends, and, soon after, most of the kids from Surfside High School hung out eating pizza on Friday nights.

Nathan told us how he came to be accepted as a *dude*. One day the manager told Edward he would have to cut his long brown hair. Citing health codes, the manager twice sent Edward home from work. The restaurant was close to having a rebellion on its hands until Nathan showed Edward how to braid his hair and hold it back with a black ribbon. Everyone was happy. Nathan became the coolest land-locked-educated-establishment geek Edward and his cronies had ever met.

The pizza that the guys gave him in tribute made Nathan grin madly. One of them had informed Nathan that they all figured he had to quit because he had AIDS. 'Yeah. You don't look so good,' Edward told Nathan. 'Take care of yourself.'

6

In mid-November, daylight becomes a precious commodity. The mornings don't begin to brighten till seven-fifteen, so seven-thirty is sufficient to catch first sight of the sun. If we see the sun that day at all. To endure the chill of dawn, I wear long johns, heavy sweats, and mittens. Early mornings on the beach, complete with winds and salt spray, are colder than any place else.

November the sixteenth, however, arrived right in the middle of a freak warm spell. When Marjorie and Katherine and I met to greet the sun, the air was already spring warm. We shed one layer of clothes and decided to go barefoot on the cold sand; it could be the last time for a while. Though Katherine thought we were asking for colds, even she agreed it might be worth it.

'It feels like Christmas,' Marjorie said as she held the door open for Odious to come out with us. I knew what she meant. We had the sense of anticipation, of a holiday. Even Miles had taken this Friday off. Nathan must have checked with each of us twice to make sure that we would keep this Friday free for him. Over the past week his happiness and excitement have filled the house like the smell of gingersnap cookies baking, and I kept forgetting that what we were doing today was gathering to celebrate Nathan's life before it ended.

'"Do I dare disturb the universe?"' Marjorie flung her hands in the air and went running over the dunes down to where the tide left the sand cold and wet. Katherine and I followed her more sedately.

'That's from T. S. Eliot, "The Love Song of Somebody or other Prudence", isn't it?' Katherine faced Marjorie. 'Half the time you don't speak, and when you do, it's just as likely to be someone else's words. If you ever have children, they probably won't say their first words until they are at least seven, and then they'll open their mouths and quote Nietzsche.'

'No, they won't,' I said. 'Haven't you noticed that Marjorie only quotes poets though she reads philosophers. Her children will quote Yeats while thinking about Socrates.'

'Very young children look like baby gerbils. Why does everyone speculate on my children?' Marjorie looked puzzled.

'It's irresistible. You'd make the most interesting parent anyone can imagine. You'd be one of those mothers who puts raisins and chocolate chips into bowls of oatmeal so that it tasted blessedly less like a bowl of oatmeal and more like cookies. You'd call it something like "Cannibals in Quicksand" and your kids would wake up clamouring for "Cannibals in Quicksand". I can see it all now.'

Marjorie raised her eyebrows at me. 'My children would eat cheese grits and live with their grand-parents.'

Katherine spun slowly, eyeing the weather in every direction. 'Forget about Marjorie's offspring. Do you think it looks like rain?'

'Tut, tut,' said Marjorie.

'Come on.' Katherine sounded impatient. 'What do you think? Nathan wants us all to have a bonfire on the beach before he leaves. He's planned our afternoon and evening around it. How does the weather look to you?'

There were clouds in the sky wherever I looked. 'I think it looks formidable.' I guess weather is supposed to come from the east, but this weather looked to be converging on us from every direction. 'As warm as it is, we could even have a thunderstorm.'

'Let's gather driftwood for a huge indoor fire, then. That way we'll have covered every eventuality.' Katherine set off down the beach.

By the time we came off the dunes with our arms full of wood, Nathan and Miles were both awake and busy in the kitchen. In front of him on the counter, Miles had a dirty-looking blob which he alternately pulled at, then ground away with the heel of his hand. He was absolutely engrossed in the blob. He put his hand into the flour bag and tossed a puff of flour onto the counter. The pushing and pulling continued.

Katherine looked astonished. 'Miles, I would have sworn you did not have a domestic bone in your body. I'll bet you didn't wash your hands first. Are you making bread?'

'Yes. And I even washed under my fingernails, those hotbeds of germs that they are. Not only is this bread, it's dill bread, and it will be broken at Nathan's dinner for us tonight. Can't you females go away? We're having a male bonding experience.'

We watched in silence. Marjorie went for a refill of her tea and got yelled at for getting in the way.

'Are you sure you wouldn't like some help?' The doubt in Katherine's voice floated on the top like grease. Nathan smiled at her and went on de-veining a huge pile of shrimp. I wondered if Nathan's strange, furry-lipped allergy to seafood had desisted.

'We shall struggle on manfully,' he said. 'Could we all meet at twilight with a pile of warm clothes in case the temperature drops? Weather permitting, I'd like to have a bonfire.'

'In this autumn time of ever-changing light, what do you call "twilight"?' Miles asked.

'Hmmn.' Deftly parting a shrimp from its shell, Nathan fished out the vein with his fingers. I used to leave the vein in shrimp before I learned that the vein is actually a shrimp's way of having a bowel movement. 'Perhaps four-forty-five. Sound good?'

We all thought so.

'Nathan,' Marjorie said. 'Penman asked me to tell you he would be honoured to supply the wine for this evening.'

'That's kind of him, but . . .'

Marjorie interrupted him. 'It would mean a lot to him, Nathan.'

'Done, then. I'll thank him whenever he emerges.'

Until early afternoon I secreted myself in the attic,

writing letters. Directly beneath me Marjorie decided to try and uncover the floor in her bedroom. Down in the kitchen Katherine read scientific journals, and Miles helped Nathan all day. Even in the attic I could smell garlic sautéing and bread baking. The day felt like an early, eclectic Thanksgiving where I didn't get to do any of the cooking.

Shortly after two, I heard steps on the stairs and Penman's head appeared, his hair damp and on end. His chin was just level with the attic floor, and I had the impression I was speaking with a head on a platter.

'Good afternoon, Penman.'

'Getting out of bed is a ridiculously tortuous experience and I don't appreciate your chirpy greetings one iota. I climbed up here to see if you wished to accompany me to a shop you might like. I'm going to spend an outrageous amount of money, and I thought you would like to watch.'

'Yes. Are we going to buy wine?'

The head stared at me. 'Are you a witch?' Not much surprises Penman, so I enjoyed his reaction. He still stared at me fiercely, though, and I needed to laugh.

'No mystery, Penman. Marjorie told Nathan you wanted to. Where are we going?'

'To a place I know. Speed is essential; I told him we would be there at two-thirty. You won't require a heavy coat. The weather has hotted up beguilingly.'

'I know. *Some* of us have already been awake for eight hours.'

'Ugh.' Penman grunted in reply, his head disappearing to the tune of descending footsteps.

We took Penman's car and Marjorie and I both went along. Katherine wanted to come, but Penman told her he could only bring two extra people. 'A minuscule place,' he said. But in the car Marjorie accused Penman of having a different motive.

'You didn't want Miles *or* Katherine to come, did you?' Penman only smiled widely, and Marjorie continued with certainty. 'They are both so careful of money that they would have taken away your fun. Feeling extravagant today, Penman?'

We drove about five miles in toward Hampton. On our left hand side was a small house in the middle of two fields. At its gravel driveway we pulled in and stopped. The only other car was an old red roadster in triumphant condition. In a just world, the man who drove it would sport flying goggles and a cap like a leather egg cosy. Beside the car, next to the front walk, a small sign announced in elegant printing Gavallan's Wines.

The door opened before we pressed the bell, and Penman shook hands with an elderly man who had a pleasant face. He suited his car.

'Mr Gavallan, it's Morton Maverin. These are my friends who are helping me to choose.'

'Good afternoon, Morton the Fourth and friends. How are your parents keeping, Morton?' It was one of those Southern questions that people always ask when they already know the answer.

Mr Gavallan didn't wait for one. He took us around to the side of the house and opened two cellar doors which led into the ground beneath the house. We waited while he unlocked a door at the bottom of the stairs. Open sesame. Then we followed him into his wine room.

'Wow.' I didn't mean for that to be audible, but it just escaped. The rooms were low ceilinged, barely high enough for my head. The walls were made of wine racks, the ceiling of smooth jewel-coloured bits of glass pressed into the plaster. Light came from green-shaded brass floor lamps, and leather chairs were set beside them. Leading us over to a table on which a small cask rested, Mr Gavallan touched the tap on the cask and held a wine glass beneath it. After each of us had a glass and he had one himself, he asked Penman what he would like.

'Two bottles of champagne, sir, and one of port. Tonight we are bidding farewell to a friend we won't see again, and I'd like something special.'

Marjorie and I sipped our wine and watched Mr Gavallan while he thought. His eyes roamed over the bottles. The room felt strange and old. Some of the bottles had parchment labels with beautiful handwriting on them.

'Excuse me,' said Mr Gavallan. He went off to a side room and brought back a dark, squat bottle. 'This is the port for you. A few years shy of sixty years old, and very special indeed. Only to be drunk with best friends. I can't offer you anything quite so grand in the champagnes, I'm afraid. Anything that old in a champagne would have gone off unless the sediment remained intact. I do have these two, however.' He reached for bottles with pink labels and dark glass. A wire nest twisted intricately over each mushroom cap cork. The bottles looked magical, and they suited the setting.

Penman and Mr Gavallan went back to the table to discuss the price of magic. After about five minutes, they walked back, both looking content. Mr Gavallan put the bottles into red felt pouches with drawstrings, and we each carried one – very gently. We had been given strict instructions not to shake the contents of the bottles, particularly the port. Ideally, we'd been told, the port would have been laid down for a few weeks after travelling even the short distance between the cellar and our beach house.

'I wish your friend well,' Mr Gavallan told us, and gave us his card. 'Give my best to your parents, Morton. Enjoy the wine. It would be difficult not to.'

We were in the car when a thought struck me. 'Too bad we've only got plastic cups to drink out of. It seems incongruous to sip magic from a cartoon character cup.' Though John Hamden had left us with a full supply of glassware mugs, wine goblets, and delicate cups for liqueur, Katherine had packed those away after Nathan had chipped one. For two weeks now our standard drinking vessels had been free cups we'd collected when we first arrived at the beach. One came free with every Big Mac Miles purchased at MacDonald's.

'Ah, but you won't be sipping from those foul things. After much cajoling, Mother sent six of Great-grandmother's champagne flutes and six crystal glasses for port. We shall drink to Nathan in appropriate style.'

Up in the front seat I was sure Marjorie was rolling her eyes. I patted the bottle in my lap and thought how we all say goodbye in our own ways. Since he meant it as a tribute to Nathan, Penman could have spent one month's house rent just as easily and more appropriately on supplies for Nathan's soup kitchen in Hampton. But I guess every goodbye has the imprint of the person who says it. Penman offered his extravagance and his enjoyment of that extravagance to Nathan and all of us. I had no doubt we could drink and smile, and tomorrow go back to plastic cups and tap water.

On the way back to the house Penman turned the windshield wipers on intermittent setting to handle the occasional drops. It was cooler now, too.

'The sky looks like raw oysters,' said Marjorie.

I couldn't say more than that about the weather. Since the definitive statement had been made, I felt free to change the subject.

'Whatever Nathan's going to tell us, he's been working on it for the past two weeks.' I was very curious about how he'd say it. How he meant to pass over his life to us. My grandmother used to tell us anecdotes of her childhood. The stories were funny and marginally revealing, the original emotions in them dimmed by time and re-telling. Nathan wasn't old enough to tell stories like that.

'He said it would be a flashback. I've been practising drowning in my mind,' said Penman. 'Even at the rate of one flashback memory every second, I'd need to flounder dramatically for at least fifteen minutes in order to relive all the apocalyptic moments of my life.'

'I think you mean apoplectic moments, Penman.' Marjorie's mouth twisted in amusement. Feeling noble after his wine spree, Penman ignored her.

We were back at the house at half past three. 'Barely enough time for the champagne to chill,' Penman fretted. He whisked the bottles out of our hands on his hurried way into the kitchen.

Only Miles still laboured over the food. A tart pan was on the counter by his side, and he was picking through raspberries and slices of kiwi to arrange on top. 'I'm playing with my tart. Leave me alone. Nathan has taken my car and gone to do some photocopying while I finish off dinner. He has outdone himself on the food.'

I wanted badly to see the contents of a huge wicker basket on the table, but Miles waved his hands threateningly. 'Get away. You'll see it all soon enough. Nathan would be very disappointed if you didn't show the proper amount of astonishment. He should be back soon. He was trying to handprint the programmes for tonight, but his fingers got tired, so he finished one and decided to make copies.'

'A programme? Good heavens. Wonders never cease,' Penman said.

I looked over at Marjorie. The last word Penman said left a silence which we both felt. Cease. Crease. If time is a sheet that flows on, then let today lie in a crease and let it stay. Cease. Crease. Please. If only the rhyme was perfect it might work. Wonders do cease, though, and they do go gently into strange nights. With any luck, this was the only useless reverie in me. Whatever else *was*, useless reveries were not a part of Nathan's programme.

Penman left the kitchen for a moment and went to root in the front closet. He returned carrying a beautiful wooden container about the dimensions of a large tackle box. With a tiny golden key and a small squeak, the lid opened to reveal Penman's old family crystal. The lid had individual compartments for six small glasses, and half of the bottom was divided to hold six champagne flutes. The other half held a crystal decanter which Penman removed so he could put his bottle of port inside. Though Marjorie was unimpressed, Miles and I were suitably enchanted, enough to mollify Penman.

'A small piece from the family picnic hamper,' said Penman airily, waving at the box.

Nathan's designated dusk was barely more than an hour away. I didn't know what to do with myself and I felt very unsettled. Nathan's programmes made me feel that way, and I wasn't sure that now was a good time to try and fathom what bothered me about them. Settling myself in the kitchen sofa, suddenly I knew what rankled. The notion of Nathan emceeing his own death. It was almost like he wasn't actively participating. But that was stupid. Who, after all, was dying?

Miles came to sit on the sofa and brought me a Coke. 'I'm glad I've been busy all day. I actually enjoyed working in the kitchen like this.'

I raised my eyebrows at him. He had always seemed happy within the narrow confines of sandwiches and taco salads.

'Yes, I know. I started helping this morning because I didn't know what to do with myself. Not going to the office felt weird. But making bread was intriguing. The results are gourmet, yet you don't have to pay astronomical prices, unless you consider how much a particular baker's time is worth. That's a sunk cost, however. By my estimates, the meal you'll eat tonight is the most expensive you'll ever eat.'

I sipped and waited for him to continue.

'Nathan's time is priceless, so the cost of the labour involved in cooking tonight's dinner can't even be calculated.'

'I think you've been reading *The Wall Street Journal* too religiously, Miles. Did you tell Nathan about this?'

'Yes. He liked the idea. He said he'd never been rich before. Do you mind if I have a quick nap here on the sofa? All this cooking stuff is exhausting.'

'Go ahead. Tell me first where Katherine is.'

'She left after you all went to get wine. Apparently her car needs fluid and her tyres need air. She's really OK about Nathan, now. We actually had a good time all together in the kitchen. Can you wake me up in fifteen minutes, please?'

My problem of what to do was neatly solved for me. Miles put his head in my lap and I couldn't move. It was better not to think, so I decided to sleep and asked my head to stir back into consciousness in fifteen minutes' time. When I was little, my mother taught me to set my internal clock, to stare at my watch and imagine the space between where the hands were and where they would be when I wanted to wake up. Then I'd imagine that time span in my brain. It usually worked. But it was always good to have a back up . . .

'Penman, could you wake us up in a while, please?'

He was reading the *Tidewater Tribune* at the table.

'It will be sooner than you think if either of you begins to snore in an irritating fashion.'

Talking to Penman right before you sleep is a good way to incur nightmares.

The lights in the kitchen were mostly off, making the air inside look nearly as dusky as the afternoon looked outside. Dressed for outdoors, we were all gathered around the kitchen table. Splatters of rain showed at the window, and the beach bonfire seemed doomed; we were, however, prepared to try if Nathan so decreed.

He looked normal. I'm not exactly sure what I expected, perhaps something more dramatic. With jeans on his bottom half and a pink button-down untucked on his upper half, he looked his usual comfortable self. On closer inspection I noted a new dark blue hair ribbon. Also, Katherine had freshly and neatly braided his hair – little pieces hadn't wisped out yet to make him shaggy. In his left hand Nathan held a sheaf of papers. His right hand rested on the handle of the wicker basket. He radiated excitement.

'There are no "stars like silvery pepper", as Penman might say that Fitzgerald said first. It's not an easy night for a bonfire on the beach, so I've laid a fire in the den.' He led the way from the kitchen down the hall. Marjorie carried the champagne and Penman his wooden box.

Filing into the den, we noticed six seats had been drawn around the fireplace. We had a bean bag, a strange low rocking chair which looked to be made out of snowshoes, and four designated fireplace chairs – triangular contraptions with tall padded backs and cushions which protruded from the floor. In the dark of the den the chairs were just mounds, and I thought of a ring of mushrooms. Moving to the fireplace Nathan struck a match. The momentary flaring revealed our uncertainty.

'Come in and sit. Penman, could we have some wine?'

Penman was delighted to oblige. Out came the key, and then his beautiful glasses and the cork of one champagne bottle. He poured for all of us, and though we weren't yet ready to drink, I touched my lip to the rim of the glass. It was so thin I thought my lip felt the vibrations of sparkling bubbles. The fire flamed brightly and provided the only light.

Nathan raised his glass. 'To ceremonies. To the pompous circumstances which mark the events of any life. To all of you. For being here.' We raised our own glasses to him and drank. The champagne tasted like golden air.

Nathan said, 'Penman, I'm honoured. Thank you very much.'

Penman nodded his head graciously and looked outrageously pleased.

Nathan handed out his programmes for the evening and lit two candles so we could read them. The room went silent with our surprise. The programme was almost an outline, and the title appeared in capitals:

ON DYING WITH THE VIVIDNESS OF LIFE

I. On Drowning
  a. with Grandma

b. in the dark
c. in the park
d. with green eggs and ham

INTERVAL – DINNER

Prawns with lemon and herbs
Chicken en croute à la Nathan
Mushrooms stuffed with crab
Baked brie with bread
Marinated asparagus, carrots vinaigrette
Tippled fruits
Tart à la Miles
Wine by Penman

II. On Falling
a. into the woods
b. with perfection
c. on hard times
d. alone

'All goes onward and outward, nothing collapses,
and to die is different from what anyone supposed,
and luckier.'

Walt Whitman, *Leaves of Grass*

'Green eggs and ham?' Miles looked weirdly at Nathan.
Nathan only smiled and waited till we all looked up
at him. I thought about signals to begin, like closing
a menu.

'Are you very comfortable?' We were. Nathan settled
further into his chair, the snowshoe model which,
encumbered with his body, swung Nathan's posterior

precisely one-quarter inch from the floor. 'I'll explain while you sip away at this round of champagne. Then, if you could set the glasses somewhere safe, we'll begin.'

I held my glass just above my lip, where the bubbles punched the inside of my nose, and waited for Nathan to continue.

'Though I have no regrets, if I did have some, they would be that I'll never have the chance to be a father and a grandfather. I wanted to tell someone my stories. Telling your children stories is the right of anyone who had to listen to his forebears tell him how they walked fifteen miles to school every day, through hurricanes. Since I've got the need to tell stories, I'm afraid you all get to listen. It's my bid for immortality.

'When I tried to decide what to tell you all, I was stumped. If a man's life is defined by moments, is it the sublime or the insignificant moment which stands out at the end? Could I relate either sort of moment to you and implant the importance of the event to me? Could it be real to you, told in the usual way? I don't think so. Related to you in the usual way, the significant moments of my life would have little meaning. You see, in the past few weeks I've realized that the real *moments* of my life have been seemingly insignificant epiphanies, small things that define *me*. These small things are the ones you should remember if I'm to live on in you. And I intend to make your memories indelible.' Nathan stopped to stare at each of us, and I realized he was also gauging the amount of liquid left in our glasses.

'Penman, don't be shocked, but it's time to down in one.' Nathan raised his glass and tipped the rest of his champagne down his throat.

'A champagne shooter,' murmured Penman. 'Ah how far we have fallen.' But he managed. We all did, then we set Penman's great-grandmother's finest carefully aside.

The room was very dark now, dark outside the circle of our chairs. Nathan blew out the candles on the hearth next to him, and now it was dark even inside the circle. The only light came from the driftwood fire, and it only reached Nathan. His hair began to straggle, with wisps snaking out around his face. This semblance of normality did nothing to bring our everyday Nathan any closer.

Were this any other time, Marjorie would have taken one look at Nathan, judged the atmosphere, and then quoted Gene Wilder in *Charlie and the Chocolate Factory*, her second favourite movie: 'There's no earthly way of knowing in which direction we are going.' Penman would have speculated on madness *à la* Edgar Allan Poe. But we didn't feel like our usual selves. And we weren't prepared for what Nathan did next. Except, perhaps, for Penman, who said he'd been practising.

'I'm going to talk about water, and I want you to relax. Get very comfortable and just listen. Clear your minds of everything, and if you have any itches, scratch them now.'

Immediately, my kneecap and the tops of both feet itched violently. I saw Penman scratch his pale wheatfield of a coiffure, and even Katherine rubbed furtively at a spot under her nose. We all scratched, then tried to relax as Nathan lapsed into a silence lasting nearly a minute. When he began speaking, the words were slow and deliberate.

'Imagine that you are floating, lying on a raft in the waves and bobbing gently with the tide. Your hands are drifting in the water and have no energy. Just drifting. And the water lifts you and lets you down, lifts you and lets you down, lifts you and lets you down.'

'Say it three times and you're a poet,' muttered Miles.

Nathan barely missed a beat. 'A crab has drifted along to snap at Miles' hand, but the rest of you are floating happily, the water surrounding you, moving you gently up and down. The water is all around you and you feel light, afloat, bobbing, the water over your feet now, surrounding you, warm and soft and you light in the water. And now the water is over your stomach and all around you, bobbing and soft and warm and welcoming and everywhere, soaking into you until you begin to feel heavy. So heavy. And now you're drifting down, the water pulling you down – so heavy and warm you feel, with all your limbs drifting. You feel so heavy that you have no desire to move, and the water is all around you. Heavy. Heavy. Sinking down and down and closed all around you, water is soaking in, and it's so heavy that your limbs can't move. The weight pushes you down and the water all around you is entering you and making you so heavy that you can't move and you don't want to.' Nathan's words were coming from a long way away, and I realized, suddenly, that I was having trouble breathing.

'Down, down. You're drowning. And now, though

the water is warm and calm and mesmerizing, you realize that there are things you remember in life and you're not ready yet to stay under the water. But it's hard not to drown, and relentlessly, in images that last seconds, but in seconds that take on the vitality of whole years, your life passes.'

And with his uncanny power that must derive from dying among us, Nathan bewitched us all. I think we were all there under the water with him in that dark room. Our time taking on the importance of his time, our breathing slightly laboured, and our minds wide open to the images with which he would leave us. And then, we weren't there at all, but on an island off the south west coast of Florida. The time moved back fourteen years, back to a late summer evening at Nathan's grandparents' home.

'It rained every afternoon from about four to five, tea time in the sky my grandma said, and my brother and sister and I loved to watch. We'd stand pressed to a great wall of glass windows, shut for the storm, which would be like Armageddon every afternoon. The palm trees shook and coconuts fell. Grandpa always told us not to stand under the coconut palms. My brother said a coconut could crack your skull like an egg.

'But after the storm the island was beautiful and we would go out to scoop the tree frogs out of the pool. The tree frogs looked like engaging peas, and at first we laughed to see them scoot around the pool. But they couldn't get out, so we scooped them out with long poles before they could tire and drown. I felt very heroic, and wouldn't allow my sister to imprison particularly small frogs in ashtrays, as she liked to do for observation.

'Sometimes, after an unusually heavy rain, the salt water in the canals was diluted enough so that fresh-water crocodiles would swim up. We were never lucky enough to see one, but we relished the tales of local cats and dogs serving themselves up as snacks for the daring crocs. Occasionally we canoed in the canals. Those were tense times, and we were always on the lookout. A possible crocodile adds immensely to the enjoyment of a canoe ride. We longed to thwack a crocodile smartly with our canoe paddles. And as my grandad instructed, we would have been careful to aim correctly for the croc's sensitive nose. My sister, a bloodthirsty little thing, was more excited about the prospect of hand to reptilian limb combat. She carried her tiny Swiss Army knife with her at all times. My brother and I respected her for being the only female we knew who would kiss a worm.

'My grandma was on the opposite end of the female spectrum, but we respected her for that, too. She was old, and very beautiful – a tall, slender woman with very dark skin and white hair piled on her head. When other kids talked about visiting their grandparents, I knew they wouldn't be seeing anyone like Grandma. She told us she was born in a cabbage patch, and it seemed a reasonable assumption. No one else was like she was.

'On nights when there was a full moon, we would meet with Grandma secretly, by the pool. We had small glasses of Bailey's Irish Cream and were very silent, listening for racoons, and trying to catch each other making noises, for our legs were stuck in the water and swirling around. Water sounds were forbidden. Like lots of kids' contests, there was no actual punishment or prize for making noise or for staying Indian-walking-through-the-woods quiet. It was a matter of pride.

'One night Grandma woke us up and there was no full moon, but she had a flashlight. "Quick like bunnies," she said, and we followed her out to the pool. She and Grandpa had put lots of plants in pots all over, but the biggest was the Night Blooming Sirius, a huge, evil, cactus-type thing which had never flowered. But it bloomed that night. We stood and watched it for a while, then went out to check for shooting stars. As long as the flower bloomed we stayed awake, each of us on a chaise longue with a beach towel over us, not to keep us warm, but as a comfortable cover in the night.

'I'd never been out all night before, and I decided I preferred the sky without a full moon. I'd never noticed the stars while the moon was out. Grandma stayed out with us all night, in honour of the flower on the Night Blooming Sirius. And I learned what kind of grown-up I wanted to become.'

The room was silent like that dark Florida night. Though the memory wasn't mine, I missed it. How can you miss something that was never yours? Somewhere in my head I felt doubly sad, missing the memory and wishing that the actual experience had been mine. What memories of mine were missable? But I had no chance to know, then, because I was still drowning, as we all were, with Nathan.

'Capture the Flag is a much better game in the dark.

You know that when you're a twelve-year-old boy. You probably know that when you're an eight-year-old boy, too. But when you're eight, girls are just boys who can't run as fast. When you're twelve, girls and games in the night take on new perspectives.

'When I was twelve all the kids in my neighbourhood played Capture the Flag each night of our summer holidays. As long as they knew where we were, our parents let us stay out till nine-thirty. And we were always at Nancy Finley's house, with its big grassy front yard and untamed back yard, complete with a hill where all the family pets got buried. My brother and sister came to play and to tease me about Nancy. All the other kids came too. There were fourteen of us on a night when nothing good was on TV.

'Nancy's house was on a main road in our suburb, and we were always being warned to stay away from the street. Nancy's poodle Precious got hit one day and then there was another mound on the pet hill. I would not have liked to meet Precious in spectral form – Precious had enjoyed biting me while he was still fleshly. I avoided the pet graveyard at night.

'While we played Capture the Flag, cars would often roll by with drunken older kids in them. One night my best friend Ronny Bain threw a dirt clod at a passing car filled with hollering kids. We all stared and then began to run as the car backed up fast, hit the Finleys' mailbox, and then stopped. A big guy hopped out of the car. He was shouting and running after our retreating figures. Probably if we hadn't run, he wouldn't have come after us. Running was an admission of guilt, and guilt makes you liable to have the living daylights punched out of you. I knew, as my knees churned furiously under me, that the big kid's pride would demand a sacrifice.

'I turned to see our pursuer head off after another figure. The guy had stopped howling as he ran closer to the house. I heard his footsteps, though, and the pound of my heart, and I hid. And in time with the desperate lowering of my gasping breath, the air became quieter around me. I heard the car drive off, but I knew the big guy wasn't in it. The people in the car had just gotten tired of waiting for him. He was still out with us, somewhere in Nancy Finley's yard.

'Being hidden doesn't feel safe when you have no idea where the thing you're hiding from is. On the stones of a walkway near my bush I heard a quiet crunch which made my heart stop. Then the noise did too. He was there. I was sure. But had he seen me? A branch snapped nearby, and I almost leaped. My whole body quivered. I still heard no sound, but the air felt thicker, like another body was nearby and compressing the air which surrounded me. Then I was sure I heard a step on the grass, and another. Someone who was trying to be incredibly quiet. I heard the grass unbend as the heavy weight of a human foot lifted off of it.

'Should I run? The noises came from behind me to my right, about five o'clock if you used my nose as noon. I wanted to look, but I knew if I turned my head he'd hear. Not being able to see was cold comfort. I just wanted to know if he was there, but I was too afraid to turn my head. It was agonizing, the worst thing I'd ever imagined.

'About 200 yards away I heard the bell ring, my

mother's way of telling us it was bedtime, time to come home. I couldn't believe she'd done that in front of the guy who was hunting us. It was like flushing the pheasants so the guy could move in for the kill. I waited, and waited, and it must have been nine-forty-five, but I could not physically move. The worst thing that had happened was *nothing* but I could not endure that. I could stand a punch in the face better than this waiting. So I stood up, and scared the hell out of a rabbit that was chewing Mr Finley's tender lawn behind me, about five o'clock if you used my nose as noon. And I never forgot my fear of nothing.'

The smell of citrus brought me out of the quiet that I had filled with my own quick memories of a pre-pubescent summer. Nathan was peeling an orange. He leaned over to the fire and twisted a piece of orange skin so that the citric acid made the flame snap. The smell was overpowering. Smells are the most efficient vehicles for memories. Someday I'll be in a dark room and the smell of oranges will carry me back to the time when I drowned with my friends. Nathan filled the silence again.

'When I was seventeen my father moved us from Savannah to New York for a year. He went to study city planning, and he took us with him because it was too far for him to commute home for the weekends. So my brother and sister and I went to New York City public schools. With our Southern drawls we might as well have been from Neptune the way we fit in. I never realized before what a big country we have.

'My brother and I ran track in Savannah, so we ran track in New York City, not for the school, but for ourselves. My brother loved how running shoes made him feel when they were tied tight. He said he could run forever. I ran because it was faster than walking and because I could see more that way.

'We ran most afternoons in Central Park. My mother would have had frantic fits had she known. To her, New York was hell and Central Park was a particularly fiery furnace. She would have made us run with a pack of Rottweilers. But at fifteen you're invincible and you don't worry about getting mugged, especially when there are two of you.

'Though I never feared the mugger's knife, the people sleeping on the park benches bothered me. Those people with no place to go and nothing to do scared me worse than gangs or drug dealers. Bag people gave me an inside scare which had components of guilt, but mainly fear. Would it be possible for me, one day, to feel no purpose and belong nowhere, and to be content to do nothing? You see, everyone always told me I was going to do great things, and I believed them. Until I saw those men and women sleeping on benches. Because I was sure that once they'd had dreams too, and then something happened and they became nothing. Many of them weren't any older than I was and they had nothing and I had everything. I wanted to assure myself that their impotence was not mine. I wanted to help, but the impulse arose less from altruism than from a sure instinct that if I could help them, I nullified my own impotence.

'Running through Central Park I soothed myself with helpful imaginings. When I was a mogul, I'd come back here and shake these people awake. I'd give them jobs and low cost housing. Money was the key to it, and I began to see lack of money as the most evil thing in the world. These sleepers had no money and couldn't get housing, no housing and couldn't get jobs. Though I knew agencies were set up to help these people, some slipped by – maybe they needed more than food and a roof. I thought they needed the idea that fate or luck was on their side. They were helpless on their own to even find a bed at night. It is easier to do nothing if you don't care.

'I imagined bringing turkey sandwiches and thermoses of coffee to my parked people. Saw myself as being that small spark which set their stalled lives in motion. All the time I was thinking of this, not just while running. If I was who everyone said I was, then I should be able to help. At least one person. And I had to do it soon, because I was becoming as helpless as they were.

'So one day on my afternoon run I stopped and sat down on a bench which was three-quarters taken up by a heap of clothes. My brother wasn't with me. He had found a girl at school by this time, and his runs through the Park were less frequent. I couldn't have explained my actions to him anyway.

'The heap of clothes on the bench was a man, and I didn't know what to say to him. So I just noticed how many layers of clothes he had – a dirty trench coat over a ski vest over a sweater and another and under that I couldn't see. It was fifty-five degrees and I had on shorts. Surprisingly, the clothes didn't smell like body sweat or alcohol, just like dirt. The man was probably more a part of the park than the bench was.

'"Would you like a soft pretzel?" I asked the space

down at the other end of the bench where I supposed his head must be.

'"Are you a damned journalist out to ask what I think of the government that leaves me like this? You can't be, they never offer food." The bundle rolled itself over and up to a sitting position. A man with a few days' beard and brown eyes stared at me. "What's up?"

'Now that I'd actually done this thing, I still didn't know what to say. The man continued to stare at me, then he stood up and began to walk over to a hot dog stand which also sold pretzels. "Come on," he said over his shoulder. Wordlessly we walked the short distance, the smell of the hot dogs drifting up my nose and making me hungry. Not just hungry, but ravenous, me who had eaten not four hours earlier. How long had my benched companion been without food? I wanted to offer the man more than just a pretzel, but I didn't know how to offer – being a kid – without hurting his pride. Telling him "Hey guy, since this is the only meal you might see this week, why don't you have a couple of hot dogs," seemed less than tactful.

'Not knowing what to say, but having to say something, I got very red in the face and told him, "Have whatever you like I . . . I . . . well, I just got my allowance today." And then I felt phenomenally insensitive for bringing bits of my privileged life out to flaunt in front of him. My cheeks grew hot like they'd been grilled, and he just stared at me.

'"What are *you* getting?" he said. I told the hot dog lady I wanted a hot dog with relish, ketchup, onions, and mustard, and a Coke.

'"Make that two," the bag man said.

'We watched while the hot dog lady piled on the neon green relish and the little pertrified onions. The hot dogs came in white paper troughs which held the overflow. I was horrified as the bag man reached in his back pocket for a battered plastic wallet. "Oh no, please, I'll pay. For both of us," I said.

'The bag man shook his head and asked the hot dog lady for a receipt. "Don't worry about it, kid. I'm on expenses, and I'll bet you're not." I had no idea what he meant, and I must have looked pretty dazed. It took a moment for me to work it out. The man, watching me, laughed.

'"You know," he said, "I've been pretending long enough so that it felt really good to be able to say that." We took our hot dogs back to the bench and with every step I was feeling more and more foolish. And, perversely, mad.

'"So you're not really a bum. Why are you out here dressed like one?" I knew I sounded hostile but I didn't care. The man just looked at me and ate his hot dog. He spoke after a while, through large bites.

'"I work for a lobbying group for the homeless. Actually, I'm based in Washington, like any lobbyist worth his salt, but the people who are paying me wanted the view of the classic Central Park indigent. I've been here a week getting a first hand view of the homeless. I keep being pestered by journalists from newspapers with democratic editors. Those guys think I'm a career bench sleeper. I don't want to talk to people from my world, though, and teasing those guys lost its fun after my first interview with a guy from some socialist rag paper. The guy asked me what I thought of the president, and I told him blearily that any president who can't give every human being a decent daily tot of rum ought to be sacked. He wrote it down like it was Wordsworth.

'"I haven't talked a whole lot to the other bums. You don't need to do that to fit in. You just notice how people look at you. It makes you feel different." The man bit down to the very end of the hot dog and then threw away the last piece of bun and the little puckery part of the meat, the part of a hot dog that looks like a belly button. I'd already finished mine, but I sat still, fishing the onion bits out of my wisdom teeth and feeling vicious.

'"So. Why'd you offer me a pretzel, kid? Why'd you come here and want to talk to someone who sits on a bench all day?"

'I don't think I replied, I just shrugged. I tended to shrug a lot when I was seventeen.

'"Those impulses to do good will destroy you. These people here, like me, or what I'm pretending to be, are not like you think. And they may hate you for your charity. It won't make you feel good. Pride's a weird thing. Were you feeling charitable when you offered me food?"

'I felt I was losing my dignity fast, which seemed terrifically unfair; all I'd wanted to do was help. I decided the best defence was to be offensive. "Why do you think it's bad to help people?"

'"I don't think it's bad to help people, but it's a waste of time trying to get people to want to help themselves. People want to preserve their status quo, whether they are affluent people who live opposite

Gramercy Park or whether they are poor people who sleep in doorways. All those repetitions of 'Let it Be' really screwed people up, I think.

'"I can see you're getting riled and want to tell me no one likes sleeping rough. I won't steal your fire, kid. You're right. Very few people enjoy sleeping rough, but even fewer people dislike it enough to want to change it. And I'm not going to give you some crap about an old hobo I met, who the social workers keep trying to stick in a shelter and who won't stay there because he likes sleeping in a box with a view of some trashcans. I don't offer that man as a palatable explanation of why some people have no homes. That man was unusual for any social strata. He liked how he lived. Even in Trump Towers I have met few people who liked how they lived. Do you like how you live, kid? Are you happy?" That lobbyist stared at me hard, very hard. I could not avert my eyes, nor could I answer him.

'I never did answer him, busy as I was with loathing him. I figured I had been pretty happy till I met him. But he must have understood the look on my face, because when he next spoke his expression had softened.

'"Look, I'm not saying it's fair, but it's not awful. This morning I woke up on my bench and it wasn't raining and it didn't look like it would rain all day. I haven't felt so excited and grateful since I was four and the tooth fairy left a quarter under my pillow. Every life has its compensations, and the ability to be happy depends on how ready you are to find them. If you want to help, kid, don't deal in charity, but in compensation. Jesus. Just listen to what sitting on a park bench for a week does to you. I needed to say that, as much as you needed to hear it. No charity. Compensations. And remember not to wear your watch next time you go running through Central Park, stupid."

'The lobbyist alias bag man left me and went off to relieve himself against a tree. I didn't see him again, though I did hear of him. A couple of months later I saw a piece in *The New York Times* which caught my attention. It was written by a lobbyist who spent a fortnight in Central Park as a bag man. The lobbyist said that the most memorable event of his two weeks was a conversation he had with some Southern kid who talked like he'd been weaned on grits and squirrel stew. The article said that it was a compensation for his stint at outdoor living.'

Nathan added a few pieces of wood to the fire. When he first finished speaking, I thought that the flames had died without my knowing it. The room was completely black. Then I noticed that the dark was my closed eyes. People drown with their eyes closed, I think, so that the backs of my eyelids can be a screen for memory's projections. Without consulting my programme, I knew what was next. Green eggs and ham.

'"I will not eat them in the dark, I will not eat them in the park,"' Nathan quoted, and then we were gone again, back to Nathan's Savannah home on the first day of first grade. And not surprisingly, Nathan didn't want to go to school.

'I was never, ever, a cute little kid with a winsome smile. Even when I was five, I was big. I think all the other kids' mothers wondered if my Mom spiked my peanut butter with steroids. Photos of me at five show

193

me taller than the kitchen counter, with a tiny head dominated by a nose like a tulip bulb. I was a boon to my sister. She was three, and people were set on taking away her pacifier. Because I was so tall, I could find that pacifier wherever it went, a talent which led my parents to call me the benevolent cherry picker. What did I need first grade for? I could read books, and, in retrieving my sister's mouth plug for her, my life had gained purpose. School was surely extraneous.

'So, on Sunday night before the first Monday of school, I told Mom and Dad I had no interest in being educated outside the home. I read to them to prove my knowledge. Other kids might have resorted to being cute and winning, but I read to them a Dr Seuss book called *Green Eggs and Ham*, because the phrase "I will not" seemed a good one to repeat. I counted on it to pound some essential subliminal sense into my parents. Besides, I loved the thought of green eggs.

'Mom and Dad were a very appreciative audience, but they told me I had to go to school. The main reason seemed to be that Mom had already picked out what I was going to wear. So I went to bed Sunday night with the knowledge of dire consequences ahead.

'Monday morning, after I got dressed, I drifted downstairs to the smell of bacon and eggs. No one cared about cholesterol back then. My brother, a veteran of elementary school on his way to second grade, and my sister, safe for another year, were already at the table. They were cackling at their plates. We were having green eggs and ham for breakfast. After that it was a tradition. Green eggs and ham on the first day of school every year. Not in the park, not in the dark, just green eggs and ham around our old kitchen table. I had green teeth the whole first week of first grade.'

Sometimes you become aware of a smile on your own face of which you've been unconscious for a while. My face hurt with smile. Becoming aware of an unconscious smile involves stepping out of yourself and looking back. I looked at all of us around the fire. Marjorie had her eyes closed, but she was smiling slightly. Katherine looked rapt, and Penman thoughtful. Miles' eyes were still closed and I peered into his face, momentarily amazed that he could have dozed off. He must have been looking back at me through slitted eyelids.

'Do you really think I could have slept through that?' Miles questioned in injured tones.

Those words broke the spell, and suddenly we were restless. Nathan lit more candles, including several I hadn't noticed on the mantlepiece. 'You've all been under water a long time,' he said, smiling at us. 'The best thing for nitrogen narcosis is decompression, another name for slow expansion. And the best way I can think of to expand is to have dinner.'

It sounded, in a long convoluted way, like a good idea, but no one moved. Some sort of acknowledgement had to be made, an acknowledgement of mental journeys and of brief trespasses permitted. Nathan's memories gripped us, and the real world seemed a little less vivid than it had before. Or maybe it was the semi-darkness of the room. Marjorie said quietly, '"The smallest sprout shows there is really no death, and if ever there was it led forward life, and does not wait at the end to arrest it, and ceas'd the moment life appear'd."' She looked down at her shoe. 'Walt, again.'

Miles directed his words at Nathan. 'That quote goes with the one on your progamme, doesn't it?'

'Yes, I like Walt Whitman.' Nathan, still seated, heaved his picnic basket closer to him in a manoeuvre composed of several awkward thumps. Spreading the basket's wicker wings wide, he began to unpack it. 'My class read Whitman's *Leaves of Grass* in eleventh grade,' he told us. 'I kind of enjoyed the poetry, though it wasn't cool to admit my appreciation once the teacher informed us that Whitman was a, gasp, homosexual. Sixteen-year-old boys are the biggest homophobes on earth.' Nathan threw a picnic cloth out to flutter down into a neat square in the middle of our circle. I caught myself leaning forward, striving for a better glimpse of the food in the hamper's insides. Nathan put two perfect loaves of dill bread on the cloth.

Penman said, 'When I was in eleventh grade, people thought I was a deviant.'

'Eunuch is more specific,' said Marjorie helpfully.

'It was just that I wasn't enraptured by football and kick-boxing movies,' said Penman disdainfully.

'And you wore hand-tied bow ties, and you only hung around with me, and you ate asparagus with your fingers, when you ate it at all. You also held your pinky out when drinking.'

'Are you saying that makes Penman homosexual?' Katherine was becoming interested.

I found it hard to concentrate on the conversation.

Nathan was setting out what looked like chicken in pastry pillowcases.

'No,' said Miles, 'But it definitely would leave Penman wide open to teasing, and I'll bet high school would have been lonely if he hadn't had you, Marjorie.'

Nathan unwrapped the plastic from a white plate with huge shrimp arranged as though they were kowtowing to a dish of lemon tarragon mayonnaise in the middle. I wanted to bestow a benevolent pat on one of the prawns' headless bodies.

Penman spoke sourly. 'If ever there were a dark but necessary time in existence, it was high school. I cannot fathom the rationale of adults who look back on those years of post-pubescent nightmare and muse sentimentally that those were the best years of their lives. If life only goes downhill after that, as many of my parents' friends claimed when they slapped me on the back after graduation from St Christopher's, we might as well all expire now with Nathan.'

'Not before dinner, preferably.' I was looking on the picnic spread with wonder, and even Penman paused from his tirade to eye the brie greedily. He pronounced it time to partake of the second bottle of champagne, which was on ice in the kitchen.

Nathan passed small glossy paper plates around. He said apologetically to Katherine, 'I wanted there to be as little mess as possible, so the plates had to be disposable.' But our napkins were cloth. They were wrapped around silverware, and Nathan took great care in passing the bundles out.

'This one's for Katherine, no, wait, Miles, and here's Penman's.' He lay the napkin by Penman's bean bag.

'And Marjorie's and, yes, this is Katherine's, and here's yours.' He put a napkined cutlery bundle in my hand. 'These are your souvenirs. It's also my will. You'll have to fit the pieces together, because I wrote my will on a bedsheet, then cut it up to make napkins. You can't look at it till I've left, though.' Nathan grinned widely. 'Let's eat.'

Penman retrieved his grandmother's glasses from their strategic points.

'Are you sure you know whose is whose?' asked Katherine suspiciously.

'My dear Katherine, my microbes are your microbes.' Penman handed a glass to Katherine and she looked momentarily bemused.

I nibbled first at the asparagus, long vibrant green spears no thicker than rose stems. The crabmeat was backfin and the mushrooms tasted of wine and garlic. Marjorie spread brie on dill bread with enthusiasm. Miles savoured a prawn and Nathan chewed carrots.

'I wanted to be able to enjoy my own funeral baked meats. It seems wrong to me that dead people can't enjoy their own wakes. Our society is very uncivilized about dying. The way people carry on, you'd think no one believed in an afterlife.'

'Unlike some individuals gathered here this evening, I'm not usually hung up on normal,' Miles said, 'but you have to realize, Nathan, that your attitude is not entirely conventional?'

Marjorie smiled at Nathan. 'You're having fun.'

Nathan looked back at her. 'And why not? There are things to be enjoyed in all this. Would you rather be keening and gnashing teeth? It's dramatic, but not very practical. Other cultures are occasionally very sensible about death. Some people actually choose their time of dying – they call everyone in to say goodbye and then they simply let go their will to live. We Anglo-Saxon Christian types tend to deal with it in a way that overshadows life. Don't mourn me very long. Better yet, don't mourn me at all. I've lived almost exactly the life I've wanted to, so be happy for me. And be happy for you, too. If we were in India of 200 years back, all this food might be poisoned so that we could be together in the rapidly approaching afterlife.'

Katherine choked on a mushroom cap. 'What a lovely thought, Nathan. I've lost my appetite.'

'More for me then,' Miles told Katherine, removing a second mushroom from her plate. Nathan just reached for another prawn. Seconds later Miles did the same.

'It'll take more than a suspicion of mass suicide to put me off these shrimps, you scheming longhair.' Miles chewed for a moment. 'Do you mind removing the fruit tart from the hamper, Nathan? I want to display my unusual slight-of-hand with raspberries and kiwis.'

Nathan cleared a space for Miles' fruit tart in the middle of our picnic. We oohed obligingly and Miles beamed like a proud parent.

'From someone who used to think that cheese and chive potato chips were the apex of *haute* cuisine, that is quite an admirable effort, Miles.' Penman nodded at the tart condescendingly. 'Technically speaking, it might more aptly be termed a flan.'

'Penman eats mass market cheese puffs, Miles.' Marjorie deflated Penman's pompous bubble. I think an invisible safety valve floats somewhere over Penman's head; only Marjorie knows where it is, and how to let the steamy air out. Without Marjorie Penman would explode someday.

Nathan put the empty dishes back in the hamper. We'd fallen on the chicken, the prawns, and the mushrooms. There was some bread left, along with a few tiny curls of sweet butter, a mound of carrots and one spear of asparagus.

'When I was planning the menu I should have realized that I was loading up on the fruit at the end. Be very careful of the tippled fruits. That blameless looking liquid is actually brandy, Grand Marnier, triple sec, and framboise. My grandmother used to make this stuff. She said it was as powerful as prunes, and 100 million times tastier.'

'This is the grandma of your flashback, isn't it?' I was fairly certain I was right. Nathan nodded.

'She didn't sound like a prune person,' Marjorie said quietly. And that was the only reference we ever made to the images that Nathan passed to us in the dream of drowning.

Miles began to cut the fruit tart. I was sitting on his right, and was sad to have to pass four plates around to my left before one could rest in front of me. Apple jelly glistened on top of the raspberries and kiwis, and my slice quivered brilliantly in the candlelight. Miles was rightly pleased with himself.

Marjorie was the first to look peculiar and stop chewing.

'Ah, what an intriguing and innovative marrying of flavours.' Penman choked and began to laugh.

Miles took a bite and looked puzzled. 'I didn't put garlic in this,' he said, chewing slowly.

'Wuh,' I said before I could help it. The garlic flavour featured very strongly, particularly in the pastry. Katherine, looking nobly pained, asked Miles where he had rolled out the tart crust.

'On the cutting board,' he said, irritated. 'I washed it first.'

'Yes,' said Katherine, 'But it's wooden, and you probably used it to chop garlic earlier. Smell your fingers, too. You used them to fit the crust into the pan.' Miles sniffed. He didn't make a face, but since he said nothing, I knew Katherine was right. So did she, and she delivered her follow-up comment with an air of triumph veiled only enough to prevent outright war. 'The smell of garlic,' she said, 'never comes out of wood, and the only way to get it off your fingers is to let cold water run over stainless steel then on to your fingers.'

Miles took refuge in scepticism.

'All right,' said Katherine. 'We'll go to the kitchen and try it, as soon as we finish your tart. I'll bet the custard and the fruits are still edible.' Katherine ate a raspberry, then a carefully scraped spoonful of custard. 'No, the custard tastes of garlic, too.' I feared violence for Katherine once Miles got her alone in the kitchen. Nathan had the same thought.

'Perhaps you could run your cold water over a spoon, Katherine, or something without sharp points.'

'Hmm.' Katherine looked blank for a moment. 'You're trying to tell me that the righteous get no thanks. Come on Miles.'

While Miles and Katherine were in the kitchen, we quickly disposed of most of the tart still left on our plates. I think my parents used to pull this thoughtful deception on many of my childhood culinary disasters. We were smacking our lips theatrically when they returned. Katherine looked smug.

Miles said grimly, 'Now that we know that old wives' witchery works, I'm going to start my windshield wipers as soon as I see cows lying down.'

'Don't be peevish. Drink some champagne. Shall we have the port now, or at a later drinks interval?' asked Penman.

Marjorie had already consumed a glass and a half of champagne, and a large helping of tippled fruit. She answered for us all. 'Later.'

Nathan picked up his programme and looked at it while Katherine continued to dispose of the remnants of the picnic. Marjorie and Miles each picked up a corner of the picnic cloth, and Katherine and I took the other two. Watching idly, Penman told us how when he was little and his housemaids Lila and Emma folded the bed sheets, he would hover nearby to throw his terrier in the middle, so Lila and Emma could fold up his dog for his amusement. We listened, and then everyone spoke at once.

'Helpful little twit,' said Miles.

'How cruel to the poor dog,' said Katherine who had never had any pets.

'Good heavens, you had an Emma as well as a Lila.' I was impressed. Having met Lila, I couldn't imagine needing anyone else.

Placing the folded cloth on top of the hamper,

Katherine then hoisted the whole thing over to the door. I took the opportunity to head for the bathroom, as Nathan's tippled fruits were of the promised potency. Fortunately, I beat the line. No sooner had I grabbed the door knob than Miles was tilting up the stairs for the facilities on the second floor.

When we'd settled back in front of the fireplace, Nathan immersed us again in near darkness. With his cheeks bulging, he blew out each candle carefully. The smell which lingered made me think of birthday cakes. Behind Nathan the flames licked busily, and I realized that he must have added more wood to the fire.

As our eyes fastened on Nathan's face, he began to speak. 'Most people, when they are in high places, fear falling. Vertigo, science calls it. But science has no name for a disease which possesses a small segment of humanity – those individuals who fear high places because they have an urge, an insensate desire, to jump. Not suicide, but their bodies feel a need to fall. And, sensibly, the brain fears the body's compelling call to fall. Shut your eyes now and listen to me.' Once again, we complied.

'You are on the high edge of a lookout in the Blue Ridge mountains. A small black iron railing is the only thing separating you from the lip of a cliff which plunges 2,000 feet down. Around you is astounding beauty and calm, and below you, far below, is a stream at the bottom of a slope of fir trees whose tops form a long flow of velvet green. And you feel like falling, maybe because you've always wanted to fly. Though your heart beats faster with fear, your feet

move forward till the tongue of your shoe is directly
beneath the iron bar, and your body leans forward,
feeling the wind and the urge to fly. The wanting to, and
the stupidity of falling both fight within you in a place
where the importance of your life is not even a factor.
And while this is happening, you slip forward, over the
edge. The part of you which always wanted to is full of
the wild exhilaration of the impossible, with the wind
created for slicing off your ears, and the will and the
want of falling, down, faster than the horrified brain is
capable of registering stone overhang and upside-down
view of wispy white cloud in blue sky.

'And your brain shrieks back to stop, stop, look what
you'll miss. Allow me, cries your brain, to hang out for
your split-second inspection the laundry of your life.
All the people, all the events so you understand that
this is what you have to weigh against falling. The
brain hasn't had time to realize that it's too late, now,
as you're flattening with the fast whistle of falling air,
to lure you back with images of life. But still they
flash for you in an inexplicable sequence of choices
as you fall. Because the trees below you are green, live
green, the first image is of green, the green of grass,
lots of lawns.

'The summer I turned ten, I mowed as many lawns
as my neighbourhood offered. I wanted a dirt bike. A
new red Schwinn Scrambler, and I wanted it with the
intensity of sixteen-year-old boys who yearn for red
Porsches. I earned money for that bike, and saved
everything, forgoing packs of gum and all the small
things kids do with money. In late November, just as
the grass lawns had to be cut for the last time before a

mild February made them grow again, I earned enough money for my bike.

'Mom took me to the store where I bought the bike with a wad of ten-dollar bills in a worn envelope. We took it home, and after Mom took a picture of me on it, I biked out for Ronny Bain's house. I had to get there fast, because it was growing dark, so I used the shortcut by the Henley's house. The shortcut was a sloping dirt trail through the woods which bordered the Henleys' lawn.

'Mr Henley hated us using that trail right by his yard, and he had told us repeatedly to stop using it. The path was the only quick way to the other side of the neighbourhood, though, so we all used it anyway, and ignored Mr Henley's threats. He seemed a mean little man, with plaid shirts which barely stuck into his pants by the time they'd crossed over his belly, and polaroid glasses which he always wore perched on his bald head. They fell off when he got mad.

'I careened toward the dirt trail, swerving back and forth to enjoy the tight control of the deeply ridged tyres, even on gravel. The path started at the end of our cul de sac. I think afterwards that the rope stretched across the trail must have registered on me, but I just didn't have time to stop. I was going too fast. The rope hit my chest, just above the handlebars. Half my bike had roared under the rope, so when I hit it, the bike just continued on and I flipped off, over my head and onto my back on the dirt trail.

'I was sure I was dead. I couldn't breathe, and my chest felt like it had been hammered. I couldn't get any air. My eyes shut, and when I opened them, it was dark, and I could hear my mother's bell ringing insistently. I tried to move, and I couldn't. My body wouldn't obey. I had only just realized I was alive when I started getting mad. Mr Henley must have known this would happen. What a rotten thing to do! I should have died, then he would have been a murderer and in big trouble.

'After I tried to stand up and couldn't, I found I could crawl, though it hurt. The bell kept ringing at my house. I figured my sister had been given charge of it, and was going at it with her usual vigour. I crawled towards the top of the path. And then I remember the bike. I couldn't leave without it. And I remembered I had to get even with Mr Henley. Torn between these two great needs, I passed out again and woke up in the hospital. Later I gave the bike to my brother. Two months after that I was grounded for a week by my father after he caught me tying a rope between the gateposts of Mr Henley's front walk. I didn't ride a bike again for ten years.'

There was no stop for contemplation now. Nathan barely took a breath before he continued. Falling is much faster than drowning. We jumped ten years, and suddenly were with Nathan at our college, freshmen year in balmy North Carolina.

'It took me a long time to realize I wasn't the single perfect person put on earth. Till first term exams of freshman year, to be exact. No one would have realized that I did not recognize the impossible, because I was perfectly modest. But inside I knew that there was nothing I couldn't do better than other people. Until I took freshman composition with Dr Evelyn Arnly. She assigned us to write an essay, and I got a D. *See me,* the paper said in red felt tip at the top, with a notation about her office hours.

'I had written on how to make the perfect waffle in the cafeteria and I had received a D and a *See me*. I was sure she'd made a mistake. I went to see her. "You have breezed through life without having learned rudimentary grammar, syntax, and coherence. Please rewrite this paper."

'I took it from her and revised it till I was sure it was perfect, and again I got a D. Admittedly I hadn't tried too hard the first time, but that second time, I had made the essay as good as I knew how. That had always been excellent before. I was truly shaken. Dr Arnly called me to her office and gave me a collection of Emerson's essays. "Learn from these," she said. I couldn't look her in the face.

'I didn't read the book all term, even before the exam, which was a single essay. She marked my exam with a D, which stuck out on my otherwise illustrious report card like a boil on Miss America's nose. That year I also learned that other people ran faster than I did, that charm could not wholly compensate for being ugly, and that I couldn't write real poetry. The shock took a whole summer to get over, and by sophomore year I was cured. *See me*. See me as I am.'

'See me,' said Nathan again. And now I did, not falling or drowning anymore, but stationary in front of the fire. He was quiet for a long time, and though there was still whatever magic that had drawn us into his dying, it was no longer in Nathan's stories. I knew that Nathan was done remembering. Perhaps, by telling us a memory of college, he had come too close to our presence in this room.

'I think we won't fall on hard times, as my programme says. At the end we are alone. I could tell you 100 other images, but I don't need to. "Twilight and evening bell and one clear call for me, and let there be no mourning at the bar when I put out to sea." And all that. I don't have the heart of a sailor, so for me the bar is a different one. Penman, let's have your port.'

It was still very dark in the room, and Penman fumbled with the lead on his bottle of fine old port. Nathan waited until we each had a glass. The port was even darker than the room, and it smelled rich. I thought of Michael Banks, who finally got to sample port on the occasion of Mary Poppin's birthday, deep under the sea.

'I can see you all thirty years from now,' Nathan said. 'You'll all settle within a few hours of Atlanta, and you'll see each other several times a year.' He examined the liquid in his glass as though reading our tea leaves. 'Penman will be a distinguished dilettante, and Marjorie a professor. She'll teach the philosophy of poets and make people see the life in words. Miles will be a businessman, head of his own perfectly managed company. You,' he said, looking at me, 'will know the law and be a judge. Katherine will be a doctor, finding cures for what ails us.

'In the future when you speak of me, I have three suggestions for a toast.' Nathan raised his glass and said solemnly, 'Don't fuck it up.' He drank then. 'You are allowed to sanitize that particular toast once the kiddies are tumbling around, but I guarantee they'll know the real expression anyway. I defy any one of you to tell me you weren't vividly aware of that word by the time you were six.'

Nathan smiled all around and tilted his glass again. 'Dollop,' he said into his glass.

'What?' We must have chorused it.

'Dollop,' he said again. 'It's my favourite word.'

We drank to dollop. Feeling civilized we sipped for a while before Miles asked about the third toast. Nathan looked at each of us before he spoke.

'Encore.' He told us. 'Encore. I would have liked one.'

'Encore.' We raised our glasses to him and savoured that sip in particular.

We stayed just like that for I don't know how long. The silence was not a bad one. We all had things to think about, and an entire bottle of a marvellous thinking fluid.

Nathan stretched in his snowshoe chair like a great furred thing getting comfortable before an even more comfortable nap. 'I think it's bed time. Thank you. Penman for your wine, and all of you for your ears. Goodnight.' Nathan stepped carefully around us and headed for the door.

'Encore,' said Marjorie, by way of a salute. He smiled at her and waved at all of us. 'Goodnight,' he said again, and went upstairs.

The rest of us went to bed soon afterwards, even Penman. As tired as I was, I still woke up some time during the night, when I thought I heard a car.

7

___

Saturday morning, early, the day ahead looked fine. As usual, Odious and I were the first to rise. She waited for me on the porch while I went out for the newspaper. Stepping carefully through dew-soaked grass that closed around my toes like a refrigerator, I was forced to revise my opinion of the day. Fine but chilly. November appeared to be getting back in gear. As I walked, I noticed vaguely that the driveway was less full of cars than usual, and it took me a moment to fumble for a reason why. Katherine's car was gone. I wondered what she was doing out so early.

Back in the house I fed Odious and went to stand with my lower regions pressed against the stove. Katherine came in, dressed for a cold beach.

'I couldn't imagine where you were. Odious and I went for the paper, and I saw your car was gone.'

'Yes,' she said, smiling faintly, with a subtlety and mystery of which I would never have accused her. 'It's still gone.' She lifted the top of the kettle and checked the water level and cleanliness inside.

I just waited. 'Yes?'

'Nathan took my car to go home. I'll take the train to Savannah after Thanksgiving and I'll join him there.' Katherine was still smiling, and she looked so peaceful. I was torn between feeling glad for her and wanting to hit her, though I wasn't sure why. She'd minded being left out even more than being left behind. To me, that suited no imaginable standard for *normal*, but who was I to add insight to injury.

It took all through my first cup of tea to realize that Nathan had said his final goodbye just the way he should have, with no fanfare and no tears. But it didn't seem right that Miles and Penman and Marjorie should find out later. I went upstairs, ready to face the wakening of Miles and Penman in a good cause. Marjorie came down the stairs as I started up.

'Nathan's gone. He took Katherine's car and went home. I think we should read his will now.'

Marjorie nodded. 'I'll get Penman,' she said, and I was relieved.

All in all, it took Miles five minutes to stretch, complain, and then emerge from the sheets. It was a relatively graceful performance, and we were soon assembled in the kitchen. Katherine had started a pot of coffee for Miles, and he thanked her. Marjorie brought our napkins in from the other room.

We began to arrange the squares on the kitchen table but the space proved too small. Transferred to the floor, the squares of cloth took a few moments of rearranging before they made sense. Nathan had used the entire bedsheet like a page, and then cut it up, so it was a matter of getting the pieces to fit. Penman stepped back from the finished product and read it to us aloud.

'"Courage, he said, and pointed to the beach cottage, rented for a year in the sun. In it you shall find my will, disposing of the few, though precious, material possessions which I leave to you. Basically, the only thing you can't have are my hair ribbons. I shall need those in the coming time of trial. Happy Hunting. Love Nathan.'"

I laughed, I couldn't help it. Only Nathan would leave us with a treasure hunt. 'Should we start now?'

Penman looked like he was pained whenever he thought hard. 'I believe it would be something very Nathan-like in which the will would be secreted, something indelibly associated with his character. Something clever. Perhaps he rearranged the spines of his hairbrush to reveal a message.'

'I'm not sure Nathan *has* a hairbrush.' Miles looked none too thrilled with Penman's early logic.

'I'm going up to his room,' Marjorie said, and Katherine followed, because it was her room, too.

Penman and Miles and I began searching through the week's piles of periodicals. Then we checked the candle on the table, in case the will was hidden in plain sight. Then we checked Nathan's shelf in the refrigerator. I saw a white slip of paper in a bag of carrots and pointed, incoherent with excitement. Miles fished it out. It was a note fastened with a rubber band around a big carrot. 'You're getting closer', the note said. Penman called to Katherine and Marjorie, who weren't having much luck up in Nathan's room.

So his will wasn't on his refrigerator shelf, or on

the milk bottle, or in the cheese or cold meat compartments. Marjorie opened the freezer and scanned the shelves. 'Banana pudding ice-cream,' she said. We all hovered around her as she took the half-gallon container out of the freezer and examined it carefully. Nothing. Then Katherine lifted the lid. Written in indelible ink, on the underside of the lid, were the words *Nathan's Last Will and Testament*. We took the container to the table and read what Nathan had written.

'*I, Nathan Coldwell Cawley of Savannah, Georgia, do in sound mind and not-so-sound body write these words concerning the dispersement of my last effects. To Katherine I leave my entire and complete collection of* National Geographic. *To Penman I leave* The Atlantic Monthly, *in the knowledge that he will glory in his own name on the pages.*

To the other three residents of John Hamden's beach house I leave The Economist, Gourmet *and* The Southern Literary Review *along with the expectation that you will know to whom goes what.*

Signed
Nathan Coldwell Cawley, November 1, 1990.

'An embarrassment of riches,' said Penman, smiling. We got five spoons and ate the ice-cream, and Katherine didn't even complain about what an unhealthy breakfast it was.

* * *

We never spoke to Nathan again, just as he wanted. Miles and I took Katherine to the train station in Norfolk on December the fifth, and she was with him when he died a few days before Christmas. She came back to the beach in mid-January, and by then I had a nightstand made out of a pile of magazines, and so did Miles.

The weather was cold in January, but Marjorie and Katherine and I still went out on the beach to see the sunrise. I missed having Nathan there. Sometimes just looking at his hair had made me feel warmer. To his credit, we cried only a little. But always after, when we were together and the occasion caused a toast, we drank to him. Encore.